THE ADVENTURES OF SNOWDEER, PLUM PUDDIN' & PURPLE MOUSE

By Randy Plummer

Copyright © 2014
Randy Plummer
Plum Puddin' Productions

ISBN: 978-1500960414

"The Adventures of Snowdeer™, Plum Puddin' and Purple Mouse"
Copyright © 2014 by Randy Plummer and Plum Puddin' Productions.

All Characters contained herein, excepting (Santa and Mrs. Claus)
Copyright © 2014 by Randy Plummer and Plum Puddin' Productions.

Snowdeer™ – Trademark 2014 Randy Plummer
Plum Puddin'℠ Service Mark 2010 Randy Plummer

Snowdeer™, Plum Puddin'℠ and Purple Mouse
Copyright © 2014 by Randy Plummer and Plum Puddin' Productions.

All rights reserved under International and Pan-American Copyright Conventions. By payment of the required fees, you have been granted the non-exclusive, non-transferable right to access and read the text of this e-book on-screen. No part of this text may be reproduced, transmitted, downloaded, decompiled, reverse engineered, or stored in or introduced into any information storage and retrieval system, in any form or by any means, whether electronic or mechanical, now known or hereinafter invented, without the express written permission of Randy Plummer or Plum Puddin' Productions.

For more information, contact
Randy Plummer, P.O. Box 1144, Branson, MO 65616-1144
plumpuddin@tri-lakes.net

This is a work of fiction. Actual people, places, companies, and products are mentioned to give the book more of a sense of reality, but all dialogue and incidents in this book are the product of the author's imagination.

DEDICATION

I'd like to dedicate this book to both mine, and Plum Puddin's parents, Darrell and Rose Marie Plummer. You continue to be a great inspiration to me, and always will. My own adventures seemed to be never ending as I grew. Snowdeer™ and his friends were inspired by and drawn from those adventures and the foundations of integrity and family that you laid with the bricks of your own love. I thank GOD for allowing me to create another adventure for Snowdeer™ and his friends and pray that HE will use this volume to enthrall children and their parents for generations to come.

I believe that God has a unique and special plan for each of us, and pray that this fantasy will inspire you to seek, discover and enjoy the mysteries of that wonderful plan.

FORWARD

Randy Plummer is from the actual small country community of Knob Lick, Missouri. Knob Lick is securely nestled in St Francois County between Farmington and Fredericktown in southeast corner of the state. Randy lived on the Knob Lick family farm for 16 years, before moving to Branson, Missouri with his Mom and Dad (Darrell and Rosie Plummer) and sister, appropriately named Melody. Together the family opened one of the first live music shows in Branson. "The Plummer Family Country Music Show" debuted in 1973, and continued entertaining and delighting guests through 1990, helping to establish this once obscure backwater, snuggled neatly into the Ozark Mountains, into the "Live Music Capitol" of America.

Though The Plummer Family presented their last live Branson show in 1990, Randy continues to entertain enthusiastic Branson guests in live venues throughout the city. After 40 years as a musical icon, Randy was inspired to give Christmas a unique new life. It was the family friendly stages of Branson that spawned the original "Snowdeer" Christmas Story and musical CD in 2011. With his own hometown of Knob Lick in cameo as the birth place of Snowdeer, Snowdeer, like his creator leapt off the pages of his Christmas story and onto the Branson stage. The pages of the original book could not contain the love and enthusiasm of Snowdeer's new companions and friends, making new adventures inescapable.

"The Adventures of Snowdeer, Plum Puddin' & Purple Mouse" is a story about friendship with a big dose of fantasy. While Snowdeer's Christmas Story introduced us to Snowdeer and Plum Puddin', this new adventure actually takes us backward in time and introduces **them** to **each other**. The friendship that is forged will serve them well as they adventure into the unknown. Snowdeer and Plum Puddin' learn that giving of themselves is the only way to help each other as new characters magically join them on their quest. We invite you to venture with Snowdeer and Plum Puddin' as they stumble upon magical elves, fantastic frogs, talking horses and singing cats. Their journey to the North Pole is inspirational and engaging as they reminisce about their homes in Doe Run, Possum Holler and Knob Lick. They soon discover that you can always be at home, even away from home, if you have your best friends at your side. This timeless story will take you home to the simpler times of yesteryear, serve up a whole lot of homemade fun, and make you yearn for your own childhood home.

While the inspiration of God, and Randy's fertile imagination have brought Snowdeer to life, we offer these latest chapters in the life of Snowdeer to you, so that you may establish his legacy.

PICTURES

Knob Lick Mountain - Southeast Missouri

Knob Lick Country Store - Knob Lick, Missouri

Randy's Hometown of Knob Lick, Missouri

Possum Hollow Country Road

Doe Run, Missouri

TABLE OF CONTENTS

THE ADVENTURES OF SNOWDEER, PLUM PUDDIN' & PURPLE MOUSE i

Copyright © 2014 ii

DEDICATION iv

FORWARD v

Knob Lick Mountain - Southeast Missouri viii

Knob Lick Country Store - Knob Lick, Missouri ix

Randy's Hometown of Knob Lick, Missouri x

Possum Hollow Country Road xi

Doe Run, Missouri xii

CHAPTER 1: MAROON AND ORCHID MOUSE AND LIFE AT MOUSE TRAP 1

CHAPTER 2: PLUM PUDDIN'S CABIN 3

CHAPTER 3: PLUM PUDDIN' REVEALS HIS SECRET W/SANTA ...7

CHAPTER 4: THE NEXT MORNING 10

CHAPTER 5: HOLY MOLY..12

CHAPTER 6: MOSS, TONGUE-TIED AND CLEARWATER LAKE...14

CHAPTER 7: TERRIE YOUNG DEER AND THE HUZZAH VALLEY FOREST 16

CHAPTER 8: KNOB LICK STORE 21

CHAPTER 9: FIXIN' UP THE CABIN 23

CHAPTER 10: PURPLE MOUSE IS BORN..................................26

CHAPTER 11: PURPLE MOUSE MEETS SNOWDEER................31

CHAPTER 12: SNOWDEER AND PURPLE MOUSE VISIT KEN-BUCK, MARK-BUCK AND HARLEY 34

CHAPTER 13: LATER BACK AT THE CABIN 39

CHAPTER 14: THREE YEARS LATER ON DECEMBER 23 41

CHAPTER 15: CHRISTMAS EVE WITH THE MOUSES AND PLUM PUDDIN'S FAMILY 45

CHAPTER 16: MAROON, ORCHID AND PURPLE MOUSE'S PLANS TO SEE SANTA 49

CHAPTER 17: CHRISTMAS EVE IN THE BARN 51

CHAPTER 18: SANTA'S ARRIVAL AT THE CABIN 57

CHAPTER 19: WHAT'LL I DO NOW? 59

CHAPTER 20: FLYIN' THROUGH THE CHRISTMAS SKY WITH SANTA 61

CHAPTER 21: DOESN'T THAT LOOK LIKE SNOWDEER? 63

CHAPTER 22: MAROON AND ORCHID MEET JOSH ELF 65

CHAPTER 23: A WHOLE LOT OF MEWS 73

CHAPTER 24: DUNNE'S CHRISTMAS BUNS AND STRIKE THE BELL 77

CHAPTER 25: THE GOOD MEWS OF CHRISTMAS 81

CHAPTER 26: CHRISTMAS CANDY CHUTES AND SANTA'S SECRET UNDERGROUND LAIR 85

CHAPTER 27: PURPLE MOUSE MEETS TASHA 90

CHAPTER 28: SANTA'S CHRISTMAS PARTY 94

CHAPTER 29: PURPLE MOUSE GETS HIS WISH........................100

CHAPTER 30: GOIN' HOME..102

CHAPTER 31: LET'S GO AROUND THE WORLD 105

CHAPTER 32:	**J HESTON COMES TO VISIT**	108
CHAPTER 33:	**OUT OF THE MOUTHS OF HORSES**	110
CHAPTER 34:	**WHAT ABOUT TASHA?**	112
CHAPTER 35:	**NEW YEARS EVE**	114
Randy at "The Grand Village" Branson, MO		120

CHAPTER 1: MAROON AND ORCHID MOUSE AND LIFE AT MOUSE TRAP

Once Upon A Time there lived a happy couple by the name of Maroon and Orchid Mouse who lived in a small country community hidden deep in the forest called, Mouse Trap. They built their houses from leaves, tree limbs, hay, straw, mouse traps that were broken and whatever else they could use from scrap to build their tiny community. They had their own dairy called, "Cheese and Things" and produced their own milk from their own herd of cattle and especially from their best friends who just happened to be cows whose names were Guernsey and Spot. They produced milk, butter, cream and cheese for Mouse Trap and the surrounding communities of Brightstone, Libertyville, Farmington, Fredericktown, Castle Rock, Syenite and Cherokee Pass-just to name a few. Their business was always fun and thriving but as time went on Maroon and Orchid began to feel unhappy and wanted to move somewhere else where they could find fulfillment and adventure.

They knew there was a lot out there in the unknown that they had not learned about yet like, Christmas for example. They had never celebrated Christmas and didn't have much of an idea what it was or what it meant. About all they knew was that people put up trees with beautiful decorations for the season and also about a little tiny Boy child being born in a stable and was laid in a manger in a land far, far away.

Then one day they packed up what little belongings they had and told their friends and family goodbye. And with a prayer for guidance, they started their trip through the forest with a compass and a dream.

CHAPTER 2: PLUM PUDDIN'S CABIN

The Mouses loved traveling and seeing new parts of the country. They enjoyed going by different farms and making friends. Some of the people would invite them in for supper while others would give them cheese to eat, or whatever else they could feast on as they traveled along.

Then one day, they came upon some signs. One sign said Knob Lick and the other said Possum Holler. They kept going and next thing they knew they had somehow gotten off the path and were standing in a garden behind a little log cabin. This place was beautiful with a blanket of green grass, cedar and pine trees and a garden filled with all kinds of vegetables and fruits planted neatly in a row. As Maroon and Orchid were soaking up the sight of this beautiful homestead, they saw a dog running toward them. The Mouses knew it was too late to run. They had been seen and their scent had been picked up by this dog!

The dog started barking loudly as he trailed toward them. When he got to them, he sniffed them and started jumping around and rolling on the ground wanting to play! A young man who had heard the barking ran out of the cabin to see what's the matter. When he saw Maroon and Orchid he said, "He won't hurt ya-will ya boy?" Then he rubbed the dog's head and they watched as he rolled over on his back letting the boy scratch his belly.

"Oh! Let me introduce myself," the young man says. "My name is Plum Puddin' and this is my dog Pinecone. Why don't ya come inside my cabin? I have a fresh batch of plum pudding I made that's hangin' on the kettle in the hearth. I can hunt you up some cheese and crackers too and whatever else for you to eat!"

The Mouses look at each other and Plum Puddin' said, "Come on! We'll have a great time. And tonight, you can stay here before you head out to...ah...where are you headed?" asks Plum Puddin'. Once again Maroon and Orchid look at each other and Maroon finally speaks saying, "Hello, my name is Maroon Mouse and this is my wife Orchid. We came from over 'round Mouse Trap and we don't know where we are going. We left looking for adventure and a better way of life." "That's great," says Plum Puddin', and as they enter the cabin Plum Puddin' says, "Make yourself at home and I'll get you some food."

While they are feasting, Maroon notices something different about his wife and says, "Dear, why didn't you tell me? I'd been so busy these past few weeks looking for a new place to settle down that I hadn't noticed." Orchid says,

"You were so concerned about where we were going that I thought if you knew we were having a child it would be harder on you." "No, not at all" says Maroon. "This is great news! Oh....but where are we going to live? You are going to need more care while carrying our baby and then we need to be settled in a home by the time you have it!" "We'll be alright dear," says Orchid. Then Plum Puddin' says, "God will make a way, Orchid and Maroon. And not only that; I want you to consider staying here with me, at least till your new one is born." Not knowing what else to do, they accept Plum Puddin's offer.

Later that night, after all bellies are full, they sit in front of the fireplace exchanging stories about each other. Plum Puddin's Daddy Darrell and his Mother Rose Marie have come over from Knob Lick to meet the new visitors. They instantly become friends and feel like they have always known each other.

As they're sitting there watching the fire's glow and hearing the crackling of the burning wood, Rose Marie says, "You're not gonna believe this!" She points a finger at Maroon and says, "Your name is Maroon, right?" "Yes, ma'am," says Maroon. And looking at Orchid she says, "And you're Orchid, right?" "Why yes," says Orchid. Then walking behind Plum Puddin' she puts her hands on his shoulders and says, "and my boy here is Plum Puddin'! You all have Purple names! I think you were meant to be family!" They all laugh as the reality of this sinks in and makes them feel closer than ever to each other.

CHAPTER 3: PLUM PUDDIN' REVEALS HIS SECRET WITH SANTA

As they talk into the night, Plum Puddin's mind drifts as he looks outside the cabin window at the sky while eating plum pudding. His thoughts are of a special secret with Santa that began some years ago. Plum Puddin' walks over to his cupboard and not being able to hold his secret any longer, he takes out a beautiful jar studded with diamonds with a special lid that has SC written on it. He takes the jar over to the others and Daddy Darrell and Mama Rose Marie look at each other knowing he is about to tell his special secret.

Plum Puddin' smiles at his mother and father and then looks at Maroon and Orchid and then begins... "I have a secret story I want to share with you. From the time I was young, I have loved Mama's Plum Pudding. She made it for me from plums Daddy Darrell picked from their orchard over in Knob Lick. I've eaten it since the day I was born and because I ate it so much, they named me Plum Puddin'."

"Now, at Christmas time, other children leave Santa cookies and milk. But I wanted to leave Santa some Plum Pudding that Mama made. They agreed that I could, so one cold December Christmas Eve night I left a jar of Plum Pudding for Santa. He loved it so much that the following Christmas he left me this magical jar studded with diamonds, with a note that said whenever I wanted to come to the North Pole, all I had to do was fill this magical jar with Plum Pudding, hold it tight in my right hand and say the magical words, HO, HO, HO! OFF TO THE NORTH POLE WE GO! And I and Pinecone would be magically taken to the North Pole to visit Santa, Mrs. Santa and the gang! I've been taking this magical jar filled with Plum Pudding along with Pinecone to the North Pole for a long time now and we always enjoy our visits with Santa-don't we boy?" Pinecone jumps up and down and barks and then rolls over on his back so Plum Puddin' can scratch his belly.

Maroon and Orchid look at each other in amazement and Plum Puddin' says, "Just wait till Christmas Eve! I plan on going again to the North Pole and I want you to watch me as I take off!" They all laugh and Maroon says, "Count me in Plum Puddin'! Orchid and I wouldn't miss it for the world! Us, "Purple People" have to stick together and we got the Plum Pudding to do it!"

They all break into laughter again and Daddy Darrell says, "Well, I'm gonna call it a night and go home. Great to meet you all, Maroon and Orchid. Lookin' forward to many years of friendship and to the birth of your little one." Mama Rose Marie looks at them and says, "You need to name this new little one something purple-just like your names. It'll be great to have another purple mouse in the family!" Looking at Orchid, Maroon says, "Yes, that's it! Let's call our new one Purple Mouse!" "That sounds perfect," agrees Orchid. So, with that, Darrell and Rose Marie say their goodbyes and head back to their cabin in Knob Lick.

Plum Puddin', Maroon and Orchid continue to stay up into the late hours talking and laughing and enjoying their new found friendship. After about 2:30 in the morning, Plum Puddin' makes them a feather bed in front of the fireplace so they will be snug and warm and then tells them good night. Maroon and Orchid can hardly go to sleep because of the excitement of new friends, a new place to live, and a new baby on its way.

CHAPTER 4: THE NEXT MORNING

The next morning, Orchid and Maroon wake up to the smell of eggs and bacon sizzling at the hearth. Plum Puddin' had gotten up early and gathered the eggs, did the milking and all of his other chores. Pinecone is lying beside the fire on his back with his leg kicking in the air dreaming.

When Plum Puddin' sees that Orchid and Maroon are awake, he says, "Good Mornin'! After we have breakfast I have something to show you." Then he says a prayer thanking God for their food and for his new friends and when they are finished eating, Plum Puddin' leads them up the wood block stairs to a special rustic room. The room has all kinds of pictures – pictures of Daddy Darrell and Mama Rose Marie, his friend Snowdeer, one of himself with Pinecone and another with himself and Santa and Mrs. Santa that was taken at the North Pole. As they continue to look around they see that Plum Puddin' has all kinds of jars he uses to fill with Plum Pudding along with big bags of flour, sugar, salt, and jars of vanilla, cinnamon and other goodies that he will use to cook with. They look and see box after box that has Christmas decorations written on them and a homemade wooden Santa and sleigh complete with reindeer and leather reins that his Grandpa Charles carved for him and his Grandma Freda painted for him. They notice the sun shining brightly through the blue gingham curtains when all of a sudden they hear Plum Puddin' announce, "This is the room I'd like for you all to stay in. It's quiet and off to itself and when Purple Mouse is born it will have its own nursery and playground right here! Mama Rose Marie can help cook and bake and embroider pillow slips and make baby clothes. She can cross stitch with the best of 'em too! Ha-ha" Plum Puddin' laughs. "Daddy Darrell will love taking Purple Mouse to see his farm and cattle, and just being the perfect Grandpa! I also have my Aunt Gaylene who can babysit and come up with all kinds of games. So, what do you say? Would you like to make this your private living quarters?" "Oh, yes, we would love it! Thank you very much!" Exclaims Maroon and Orchid together.

So the rest of the day Maroon, Orchid and Plum Puddin' plan how they will turn this room into their personal living area. Orchid takes a feather pen and jots down a long list of things they will need and then off they go to the Knob Lick General Store to get their goodies.

CHAPTER 5: HOLY MOLY

As they make their way toward Knob Lick, they come across a good friend of Plum Puddin's. He's a mole and they call him, Holy Moly. His real name Is Donn Mobley Moly and he is the preacher at the Knob Lick Church on Molehill. Plum Puddin' introduces Maroon and Orchid to him and asks him how he's doing. Holy Moly says, "Doin' great Plum. Mama Moly is doing great too! The other day I did a marriage ceremony and someone from the congregation shouted out after they said, "I DO" that I had performed, Holy Matrimoly!" Ha,ha! They all break into laughter and then Holy Moly says, for a joke, "My little brother Guacamole turned over the outhouse while Sister Vivian was a sittin' in it and now he's grounded. Get it? A mole-GROUNDED? Ha Ha! Hey Plum, Maroon and Orchid, Come to our outdoor singin' and dinner on the ground over in the clearing over at Buckhorn this coming Sunday afternoon at 2 o'clock right after Church. We'd love to have you. Bring your guitar and Darrell and Rose Marie and Snowdeer AND some Plum Pudding." "Ok, I'll be there," says, Plum Puddin'. "Us too" says Maroon and Orchid. "Great! See you then" says Holy Moly. "Well, I gotta get back to the Church and get the outhouse set back up straight! You should have seen Sister Vivian's face when she came out of that outhouse! I thought I would be performing a funeral for Guacamole! Ha Ha! You all take care and God bless. See Ya Sunday!" "Ok, Bye Holy," says Plum Puddin' and they all laugh and continue walking to Knob lick.

CHAPTER 6: MOSS, TONGUE-TIED AND CLEARWATER LAKE

They continue on their way still laughing about Holy Moly and his family and what fun they'll have Sunday when they get together for the Singin' and Dinner On The Ground. When they look ahead they see a beautiful sky-blue lake. "This is Clearwater Lake, the clearest and cleanest lake in this part of the country" says Plum Puddin'. "I've fished and swam and in the wintertime ice skated here many times." All of a sudden they hear a loud "ribbit" and a big splash. They look around but don't see anything. They hear another "ribbit" and another big splash and they miss it again. On the third time they hear two loud ribbits and two loud splashes but this time they get water splashed on them! Plum Puddin' laughs and says, "I bet I know who it is! Moss and Tongue-Tied, You git up here on a Lily pad and talk to me or else I'll get my buddies and we'll go giggin' for Ya!" Ha Ha! They watch as two large bull frogs eyeball them from just above the surface of the water and then hop real high and land on a big lily pad right beside Plum Puddin.

"Moss and Tongue-Tied, I'd like for you to meet my friends, Maroon and Orchid." "Nice to meet you," they say. Then Moss says, "I'm Moss Ribit and he's Tongue-Tied Ribit, my half-brother. I say "half" brother 'cause I won't claim all of him as my brother" laughs Moss. "Our other brother,

Ribit Ribit is somewhere in the lake, probably eating bugs and crickets." "Must be nice to be able to eat what 'Bugs ya,'" says Plum Puddin'! Ha, ha, ha They all laugh and Tongue-Tied says, "Yes, we've been doing that ever since we were little warts!" They laugh again and Moss – not to be outdone jokingly says, "Tongue-Tied doesn't always say the most, so sometimes I look at him and say, Has the cat got your tongue?" Ha, ha, ha They all laugh and Tongue-Tied says," I thought I was gonna croak at that one!" Ha, ha, ha They all bust out in laughter and then Plum Puddin' says, "Hey, I want to let you know that Holy Moly has invited us to an outdoor singin' and dinner on the ground this Sunday. It's gonna be over in the clearing over at Buckhorn after Church. Come on over and join us!" "Ok, thanks, we'll be there," says Moss and Tongue-Tied. Plum Puddin' then looks up at the sun and sees that the day is going by fast and that they had better get on their way to Knob Lick. They say their goodbyes to Moss and Tongue-Tied and as they walk off they hear the laughing of the two frog brothers followed by two loud splashes in the water.

CHAPTER 7: TERRIE YOUNG DEER AND THE HUZZAH VALLEY FOREST

"Hey, Maroon and Orchid, we gotta make another stop before we get to Knob Lick" says Plum Puddin'. "My friend Terrie Young Deer and her family live over in the Huzzah Valley Forest. They're Native American Cherokee Indian and we have been friends all our lives. She goes by Terrie or Young Deer or all three words put together, so feel free to call her whatever of that you want!" "Ok, let's go see her," says Maroon and Orchid and off they go.

Plum Puddin' then says, "We might be seein' some of Terrie's friends along the way if they're not busy on the water. Her friend Meramec loves to canoe. He has taken me many times floatin' the rapids of the Meramec River – the river he was named after. Taneycomo his brother is also great at canoeing and has taken me a lot on the cold waters of Lake Taneycomo over there in the Branson Ozarks." "Branson?" Asks Maroon. "Yes, Branson," answers Plum Puddin'. Its west of here and a great place to visit! They got all kinds of things to do and see. Lots of Ozark music and eatin' places and fishin' and swimmin' holes! Why, if I get money enough, I wanna put me a log cabin over there to stay at in the summer and build a barn to play and sing music in and have folks come from all over to see it! I've thought about callin' it, Barn Dance Hoedown! Whooo Hooo! Swing your partner!" Ha Ha! "Don't do that Plum" says Maroon. "Something like that would never catch on." "You never know Maroon, You never know" says Plum Puddin'. "I may do it someday and I'll tell ya I told you so! Ha Ha!"

They keep walking and finally reach Huzzah Valley. Terrie Young Deer is outside her tepee beside the creek on her knees doing the wash. Her dog Prince is sitting faithfully beside her watching them as they get closer. "Terrie Young Deer, how are you?" Asks Plum Puddin'. "Doin' great Plum" she answers. "Doin' the wash and getting ready to gather berries, nuts, fruits and vegetables for the upcoming Huzzah Valley Horn of Plenty Harvest Festival. They'll be giving out ribbons on the best arrangements and I enter the contest every year. I've even won blue ribbons before." she laughs. "My friend Niangua is coming over and we are gonna do the pickin' and then have it all ready for the show next week." She quickly changes the subject and says to Plum Puddin' and all, "I am sorry I didn't ask who your friends are. Who are these fine folks?" "This is Maroon and Orchid Mouse, Terrie. They were passin' through Possum Holler and didn't have a place to stay so I invited" "Wait" says Terrie. "Mrs. Mouse, are you going to have a little one?" "Why yes, Miss Deer. How did you know?" "I have a very good sense about people and things around me. It's a God given gift of discernment. You know with your names and Plum Puddin's name all having to do with purple, you should name this baby Purple Mouse!"

"Ah-Ah-Ah" stutters Plum Puddin'. "You ain't gonna believe this Miss Terrie, but Purple Mouse is the name Maroon and Orchid have already given this little one. Matter of fact, my mother Rose Marie came up with the idea of Purple Mouse! Ha-ha!"

"Whoa! I think that's the name it's supposed to be called for sure!" Terrie Young Deer says. They all laugh and Plum Puddin' says, "Yea, I think so too! Terrie. Will you come to see it after it arrives?" "Oh yes I will for sure" she says. "Niangua and I will be sure to visit and not only that, we will make a full beaded Indian headdress and outfit for it! Also, I want to give your new one an Indian name if I may, Maroon and Orchid?" "Oh yes, we would be honored," they reply to Terrie. Then Terrie continues, "Its Indian name is Lucky Clover and it means, "God's blessing" and that is what it will have all the days of its life. And it's going to be the biggest, healthiest, fun loving, cheese eatin' boy mouse you have ever seen! Ha Ha   He will love Plum Pudding almost as much as, You Know Who." she said, glancing over at Plum Puddin'. "My my, says Maroon, this has been quite the eventful time here lately!

We've gotten new friends, a new home, new baby on the way and now we know what our new youngin' is gonna be plus his name and Indian name! We are really thankful to you and to God." Then Plum Puddin' says, "Young Deer, thank you. And I have a name I want to give to you from us. It's, "Cornucopia," meaning, many blessings pouring out." Terrie Young Deer fights back tears and Maroon and Orchid say the name fits her perfectly.

Just as they are preparing to leave, they hear in the distance a voice saying, "Wait! Don't go!" They turn around and see a canoe floating on the Huzzah River. It's Meramec. Plum Puddin' and Terrie Young Deer's friend. He's seen Plum Puddin' and with strong arms he paddles swiftly toward the gang. When he reaches the shore, Meramec gets out of the canoe and greets Plum Puddin' and Terrie Young Deer and meets Orchid and Maroon. They eagerly tell him about their trip and their new baby on the way and his Indian name. Meramec and the Mouses become fast friends and he promises to come and see the new baby mouse when he is born. Then he promises that when Purple Mouse gets older he will take him out in his canoe. Plum Puddin' looks up at the sky and asks Meramec what time it is. Meramec looks up and then says, "2 o'clock in the afternoon." After hearing this, Plum Puddin' says they should probably get on their way to Knob

Lick to buy things at the General Store so the Mouses can fix up their room in the cabin. Meramec says he wants to give a gift to them for the new one. It will be a fur blanket that he will make himself. Orchid and Maroon are thrilled to know Purple Mouse will have a new fur blanket so they thank him and say their goodbyes and then go on their way.

CHAPTER 8: KNOB LICK STORE

They finally make it to the Knob Lick Store. When Mr. & Mrs. Bailey, who own the store hear that the Mouses are new to the area and that Orchid is going to have a baby, they quickly help them with all they need. When they learn that Plum Puddin' is fixing up a room upstairs in his cabin that is especially for them, they give them logs and nails to make a rocker for Orchid and Maroon to rock their baby to sleep in and also enough logs to make a baby bed and other furniture. When Maroon and Orchid ask how much they owe, The Bailey's quickly reply, "Nothing. It's a baby gift for you and your new one." They thank the Baileys and then look at their new heap of treasures. They look at one another thinking, how are we going to get all of this back to the cabin? Plum Puddin' had forgotten to bring a wagon to haul things in.

As they are thinking about what to do, one of Plum Puddin's friends from over at Elephant Rocks, whose name is Todd Lott, saw what was happening. He says, "Hey y'all, I have exactly what you need. My horse and wagon is right outside and I have plenty of daylight to take your things to Plum Puddin's cabin and get home before sunset." "Thanks Todd," says Plum Puddin'. So they load up Todd's wagon and Pinecone jumps in between Todd and Plum Puddin'. Then Todd hollers to his horse, "Let's go Glister!" and Glister takes off. In a short while they are back at Plum Puddin's cabin and all the supplies are unloaded on the cabin porch. They thank Todd and as he rides off, he says, "If y'all ever need a ride to Branson- just give me a holler. I'm always goin' down there and would enjoy the company." "Ok," they answer back and watch as Todd starts singing a song about Branson as he and Glister disappear in the forest.

CHAPTER 9: FIXIN' UP THE CABIN

"Alright, now we got everything we need," Plum Puddin' says. "Yes, we do," Says Maroon. "So let's start now, 'cause I can hardly wait!" "Me either," says Orchid. As they start to pick up logs to cut to make Purple Mouse's rocker, they happened to look over across the hill and see Darrell and Rose Marie walking toward them. They see Plum Puddin's big pile of wood and supplies and they offer to help. "We can use all the help we can get! Thanks!" says Plum Puddin'. So they all get right to work. The men measure and saw logs and the women-folk take feathers and cloth to make feather beds for Purple Mouse and Maroon, and Orchid too. Plum Puddin' says, "Hey, while you're at it, would you make me a featherbed too? I've worn the old one out and I need a new one. I got feathers stickin' out of mine and every once in a while during the night I get woke up by one of the feathers tips! Ha Ha." "Ok, we'll make you one, but the baby bed comes first," Rose Marie says and laughs. By nightfall the featherbeds and baby bed and rocker have all been built. "Next, we need to build a couch and chairs and a table to put a pitcher and water basin on," says Darrell. I already have it planned in my head what to do and we can work on that tomorrow." "I'll make the chicken and dumplin's tomorrow while you're doin' that," says Rose Marie. "And I'll crochet some rugs and a baby blanket," says

Orchid. Exhausted from the day, they all fall asleep there in Plum Puddin's cabin wherever they can find a comfortable place to lie down.

The next day they get back to work and get everything done. Even Plum Puddin's feather bed! As they look around seeing the work they've just finished, they hear Rose Marie ring a dinner bell downstairs and shout, "Suppertime! Chicken and dumplin's are ready!" They rush downstairs and sit at the table. After Plum Puddin' says grace they all eat till their heart's content. Plum Puddin' asks, "Mama, did you make Plum Pudding by any chance?" "Yes, dear, I sure did." answers Mama Rose Marie. "I knew you wouldn't let me down." says Plum Puddin'. They spend the rest of the night laughing and telling stories and Plum Puddin' eats his Mamas Plum Pudding the rest of the night.

"Plum Puddin', would you tell that story again about you and Santa and the magical jar please?" asks Maroon. "Sure." says Plum Puddin'. "I never get tired of telling it." So, Plum Puddin' not only tells the story, he goes to the cupboard to once again bring out the magical diamond studded jar he uses every year to fill with plum pudding to take to Santa. Pinecone jumps up and down and starts barking when he sees the magical jar because he knows what it means. Plum Puddin' sadly says to Pinecone, "I'm sorry Pinecone. We aren't going to the North Pole tonight. But it won't be long boy!" Pinecone understands and goes to lay down with his tail still waging knowing that the time will come when he will make that magical trip with Plum Puddin'.

Plum Puddin' says, "Maroon and Orchid, This Christmas if you have a special Wish List you would like hand delivered to Santa, just give it to me and I'll take it to him."

"Really?" asks Maroon. "You bet! It's fun and Santa loves it!" says Plum Puddin'. And when Purple Mouse is born, I'll take his Wish List to Santa too!"

CHAPTER 10: PURPLE MOUSE IS BORN

Fall has arrived, and the leaves have turned beautiful colors in the Possum Holler forest. But something even more wonderful is happening. Orchid wakes Maroon late in the night telling him she is about to have the baby! Maroon jumps up out of bed and runs around the room saying, "What do we do? What do we do?" Orchid says, "Dear, go get some water and a blanket and we'll wait for our new one to be born."

So, in the early morning hours just before dawn, with only the light of a candle, Purple Mouse was born. "What a beautiful baby," Maroon says. "Yes, he is," Orchid agrees and then says, "God gave us a son, and I am so thankful!" "Oh, I am too," says Maroon. So they sit there together admiring their new gift from God and saying a prayer of thanks.

"Wait 'till Puddin' and Pinecone find out," says Maroon. "They'll be so excited and I bet the first thing he gives Purple Mouse is Plum Pudding!" laughs Maroon and then he asks, "Can I hold him?" "Sure, He's yours too," laughs Orchid. "I'm so thankful he was born in this safe cabin and thankful that he will have lots of friends around him," says Maroon. When he looks back down at Purple Mouse, he sees Purple Mouse looking up at him and giving him a smile. Maroon says, "Did you see that? He grinned at me!" "Yes, I saw it dear," answers Orchid. "And you'll be seeing a lot of that in the future." After holding him a while and watching him go to sleep, Maroon gives Purple Mouse a kiss on his forehead and then a kiss to Orchid. Then he hands their new baby back to Orchid, and goes downstairs to tell Plum Puddin' the news.

Maroon knocks on Plum Puddin's bedroom door. A sleepy Plum Puddin' opens the door standing in his long handle underwear with a lit candle and asks, "Is anything wrong?" "No, nothins' wrong Plum," says Marooon. "I came downstairs to let you know Purple Mouse has been born! Wanna come upstairs and see him?" "Oh yes Maroon!" answers Plum Puddin. Pinecone jumps up and down and they head up the stairs to find the new one wrapped in a crocheted blanket held by his beaming mother who made it.

"What a beautiful boy," says Plum Puddin'. Pinecone whimpers as he goes up to inspect the new baby. "Can I hold him?" asks Plum Puddin'. "Why sure you can. You're his Uncle Plum!" laughs Orchid. "Yes, I am and a proud uncle at that!" laughs Plum Puddin'. "Wait till I tell Daddy Darrell and Mama Rose Marie! They'll be so excited! After I do my chores I'm gonna head over to Knob Lick and tell them." "You'd better wait a while." says Maroon. "It's still dark outside!" They laugh at Plum Puddin's excitement and then Plum Puddin' says, "Alright, I'll go back down and try to go back to sleep 'till the sun comes up and then go tell them."

Plum Puddin' wakes up at the crack of dawn hearing the rooster crow and he immediately starts thinking about Purple Mouse being born. He laughs to himself and pets Pinecone on the head and says, "Let's get the chores done boy and then we'll go tell our family and friends!" The first place they go to is his Daddy Darrell and Mama Rose Marie's cabin at Knob Lick. Daddy Darrell and Mama Rose Marie are both so excited, they decide to go right then to see Purple Mouse while Plum Puddin' goes to tell the others. Plum goes by the Bailey's Store at Knob Lick and sees his friend Todd Lott there again. The Baileys are so excited that they close their store so they can go see the new one. Todd once again offers his wagon so he can take everyone to Plum Puddin's cabin. They all jump in and Pinecone sits between Plum Puddin' and Todd Lott. As they head to Possum Holler they stop to see Holy Moly, Tongue-Tied and Moss who all want to hop on the wagon to go see Purple Mouse. They go by Huzzah Valley and tell Terrie Young Deer, Niangua, and Meramec the good news. Taneycomo is there and wants to go with them to see this new one he has heard about. Everyone but Meramec gets in the wagon. He goes into his tepee and returns with a leather skin blanket he had promised to make for Purple Mouse, along with a full headdress outfit made by Terrie Young Deer and Niangua. They also bring along a horn of plenty full of fruits and vegetables to give to Orchid and Maroon.

As they arrive at Plum Puddin's cabin, the midday sun is shining bright on this beautiful fall day. Plum Puddin' and Pinecone race upstairs first to see the new baby again while Plum Puddin' says to Maroon and Orchid, "We have company outside. Would you care if our gang of friends comes up to see him?" "No, we don't mind at all. Please have them come up," says Orchid.

So all of them come up the stairs and stand in the doorway admiring Purple Mouse. Terrie Young Deer, Niangua, and Meramec present their gifts to him and Orchid and Maroon. Darrell and Rose Marie had already given Purple Mouse a sleep gown with the name, Purple Mouse embroidered in purple thread that Rose Marie had sewn herself.

The bond of friendship that filled the room made everyone teary eyed with no one wanting to leave. Purple Mouse looks up and seems to understand what's happening. He gets a big smile on his face and goes from one person to another grinning his big grin! "Look at Purple Mouse! Says Terrie Young Deer. He's smiling! He can feel the love and is already responding to it. He is special!" And to that comment, all agree as they watch the new member of the family.

CHAPTER 11: PURPLE MOUSE MEETS SNOWDEER

Purple Mouse loves being raised in the cabin and Plum Puddin' and Pinecone become best friends with him. Daddy Darrell and Mama Rose Marie become like grandparents. Daddy Darrell loves taking Purple Mouse around to see others that live in Possum Holler, Knob Lick and the Huzzah Valley area. He also loves taking Purple Mouse to see his farm and his cattle and lets him feed them hay and grain. Taneycomo and Meramec take him out in their canoes and Terrie Young Deer and Niangua keep him healthy with fruits, nuts, and vegetables. Tongue-Tied and Moss are his swimming buddies and Todd Lott takes him for rides on his wagon pulled by his horse Glister to visit the Knob Lick store. Todd would always buy Purple Mouse cheese and candy and he would eat it on his way back home to the cabin. While they all have a great time together and share everything, Maroon, Orchid, and Plum Puddin' have agreed that they won't tell Purple Mouse about Plum Puddin's secret with Santa until he got older. So when the time would come for Plum Puddin' to go see Santa, Maroon and Orchid would make excuses to have Purple Mouse go upstairs or wait till he had gone outside to play or take him to Plum Puddin's folks house and then Plum Puddin' would take his magical jar and leave for the North Pole.

When Purple Mouse gets old enough to go around by himself, he wanders deep into the woods and finds the sign that marks the forest of Doe Run. Being filled with curiosity and an endless love of adventure, Purple Mouse heads into the Doe Run forest. As he comes into a clearing he sees a beautiful young white deer with what looks like his mother and a buck standing beside him. There are also two other deer there with them.

Purple Mouse gasps at seeing them with the little solid white young buck. One of the deer hears him and looks over and sees Purple Mouse. "Please come over. Don't be afraid," the buck says. "I'm Jim-Buck and this is my wife Deerlores. This is our little buck Snowdeer and his grandparents Lester and Evelyn Whitetail-or as Snowdeer calls them-Papa and Mommom Whitetail," Jim-Buck laughs. Purple Mouse is still afraid and with his voice shaking says, "Hello, I'm Purple Mouse." "Pleased to meet you Purple Mouse," says Jim-Buck, Deerlores and the Grand deer. Snowdeer and Purple Mouse look at each other and then Snowdeer breaks into a smile at Purple Mouse and says, "It's nice to meet you Purple Mouse. Can you stay and play? Please?" When Purple Mouse hears that, his nervousness melts away and he feels inside that they will be great friends. "Sure. I would love to stay and play," says Purple Mouse. So the parents and grand deer watch as Snowdeer and Purple Mouse walk off into the woods talking and laughing and building a great friendship together.

CHAPTER 12: SNOWDEER AND PURPLE MOUSE VISIT KEN-BUCK, MARK-BUCK AND HARLEY

"Where are you from?" asks Snowdeer. "Possum Holler. Over by Knob Lick," says Purple Mouse. "I was born in a log cabin that belongs to Plum Puddin'". "Plum Puddin'?" Snowdeer says. "I do know him but it has been a while since I have seen him. Hope to see him again someday. Hey, you wanna meet some more of my friends?" asks Snowdeer. "Sure," says Purple Mouse. "Ok, I got my Uncle Ken-Buck who is great and he's always comin' up with these great inventions! His brother, my Uncle Mark-Buck is really smart too and they have a factory over in the Seymour Forest. They have this new invention called, Pine Cone Chips where they put nuts and chocolate together on a waffle chip that is shaped like an ice cream cone! Talk about good! They always let me eat some of them when I come over to visit." says Snowdeer. "And they're great when you dip them in ice cream! I've even picked some of the nuts they use to make them!" "MMM-MMM-MMM" says Purple Mouse. "Do you think they would let me eat some if we went over there?" "Sure, says Snowdeer. Let's head over and see if they have any free samples!" They both laugh and take off running through the forest toward the Seymour Woods.

As they arrive, they peek in the window and see Uncle Ken-Buck and Uncle Mark-Buck hard at work in their factory. They see Snowdeer and Purple Mouse and come over to greet them. "Hello ole boy," Ken-Buck says to Snowdeer. Then Mark-Buck laughs and says, "Hello Snowdeer. Did you come to work today?" "Ah-Ah...well..." Snowdeer says and then Ken-Buck and Mark-Buck laugh and Snowdeer says, "I have a friend I want you all to meet. This is Purple Mouse. Purple Mouse, this is Uncle Ken-Buck and Uncle Mark-Buck!" "Nice to meet you," they say. "Nice to meet you too," says Purple Mouse. "Where are you from Purple Mouse," they ask. "I'm from Possum Holler and live with my parents in Plum Puddin's cabin there," answers Purple Mouse. "Plum Puddin'! Yea, we know him but I haven't seen him in a while or his daddy Darrell or mama Rose Marie. How are they?" Ken-Buck asks. "They're doing great. They are the only family I know because my parents moved away from Mouse Trap before I was born," says Purple Mouse. "Mouse Trap, hmm...I've never been there, but I've heard of it. Don't they have a dairy and cheese factory there called, Cheese and Things?" asks Mark-Buck. "Yes sir they do." answers Purple Mouse. "I hope to go someday to see it. Hey, maybe you and Snowdeer can take a trip over there with us, to see it." says Mark-Buck. "That sounds great-let's plan on it," says Ken-Buck. "I'm always open to new ideas and maybe we could do business with them someday. You never know. We might work with them and make Cheese Cone Chips!" he laughs. He picks up two baskets and asks Snowdeer and Purple Mouse, "Would you boys care to pick some nuts for us please? We're just about out of them and we need more so we can finish our new batch of Pine Cone Chips to send over to Cherokee Pass. The hickory and pecan trees are over in the grove by Taum Sauk Mountain and they're loaded this time of year." "Yes, sir we sure will!" they say. "Thanks a lot, says Mark-Buck. It's a pleasure to meet You Purple Mouse." "Yes, thanks a lot", says Ken-Buck. "Nice to meet you and we'll see you after while". So the two new friends leave to go to Taum Sauk Mountain to pick nuts with their mouths watering just thinking of how good the Pine Cone Chips will taste when the two uncles get them made.

As they arrive at Taum Sauk Mountain, they see a farmer there already picking from the trees. As they get closer to him the man says, "Hello boys. I'm Harley and I came over from Ironton to pick nuts for the family. You boys new here?" "No, I've been here before." says Snowdeer. "But this is Purple Mouse and it's his first time here. My name is Snowdeer and we come from the Doe Run and Possum Holler area. My Uncle Ken-Buck and Uncle Mark-Buck have the Pine Cone Chips factory over in the Seymour Woods. They bake waffle chips and then put chocolate and nuts on top and they sent us over here to pick nuts." says Snowdeer. "You won't have any trouble finding nuts here." laughs Harley. "I come here every year and have never failed to find an abundance of them." Harley starts pointing and says, "Over here is the Pecan trees, and on this other side is the Hickory nut trees. What one do you want to pick from?" "Both," says Purple Mouse. As they begin picking, they hear Harley singing and humming, and Snowdeer says to him, "You're really a great singer. You need to be singing in one of those country music barns!" "I'm hoping to do that someday Snowdeer." Harley replies. Then Harley sees that their baskets are brimming with nuts and he says, "That didn't take you long!" "Yeah. I can usually fill a basket fast, 'cause I know how good it's gonna taste after I get them back to my uncles' factory!" says Snowdeer. They all laugh and then he says, "Well, I guess we should get going Purple Mouse. Chocolate is waiting!" he laughs. Then Purple Mouse and Snowdeer tell Harley goodbye and to keep up the great job singing. Snowdeer says, "If you are ever in one of those shows, we promise to come see you." "Thanks a lot. I'll be looking for you." says Harley. So, Snowdeer and Purple Mouse start back to the Seymour Woods. When they get there, Ken-Buck and Mark-Buck meet them at the door. After seeing the two full baskets Ken-Buck says, "Well done boys!" Mark-Buck asks, "Wanna stay for a sample?" "OOO-Yes!" both Snowdeer and Purple Mouse reply! So after they get the nuts stirred into the chocolate and pour it on top of the waffle cone, they get to try them. They're oohing and aahing and Ken-Buck and Mark-Buck send a big bag with them to eat along the way, along with some bags to take to their folks. After they leave, Ken-Buck looks at Mark-Buck and says, "What do you bet there won't be any left for their parents to eat!" Mark-Buck laughs and replies, "I'm pretty sure there won't be." Then they both laugh and go back into the factory.

CHAPTER 13: LATER BACK AT THE CABIN

Later that day at sundown when Purple Mouse arrives back at Plum Puddin's cabin, Maroon and Orchid ask how his day went and if he made any new friends. Purple Mouse answers, "Yes, I did! I met this solid white young buck by the name of Snowdeer and his Mom and Dad and his Granddeer! They live in a cabin over at Doe Run. Then Snowdeer and I went to see his Uncle Ken-Buck and his other Uncle Mark-Buck who have a factory in the Seymour Forest called, Pine Cone Chips. They were making a batch of Pine Cone Chips when we got there but they were running out of nuts so they asked Snowdeer and me if we would go nut picking! We took baskets and they sent us to Taum Sauk Mountain where there are gobs of nut trees! We picked pecan and hickory nuts and in no time we filled the baskets! We met this man by the name of Harley who was also nut picking. He would sing while he was picking and he has a great voice. Snowdeer and I really enjoyed listening to him sing and talk. And he was one of the nicest guys too! Then later when we got back to Seymour, Ken-Buck and Mark-Buck added the nuts we picked with a batch of chocolate and we got to sample some of them." Purple Mouse remembers that they had sent some Pine Cone Chips to their parents to eat but decides not to tell them because he and Snowdeer had eaten them all! Then he says, "Snowdeer and I are planning to go back again sometime to help them and to eat some more of their delicious Pine Cone Chips." "It sounds like you had a great time son." says Maroon. "Yes sir, it was a great day! I love adventure, and this whole forest is loaded with it!" laughs Purple Mouse.

Plum Puddin' who had been listening to the conversation says, "Purple Mouse, I met Snowdeer and his mother Deerlores and his daddy Jim-Buck and his Mommom and Papa Whitetail before. What great deer they are! I would love to see them again. Maybe some Christmas we can all..." Purple Mouse breaks in and says, "That's what I told them Plum!" "Did Jim-Buck or Deerlores have any interesting stories about Christmas they shared with you?" asks Plum Puddin'. "No, they didn't" answered Purple Mouse. "But I could tell they love Christmas! I noticed they looked at each other a lot while they were talking about Christmas and smiling a lot. They must be big Christmas lovers. Why do you ask?" asks Purple Mouse. "I was just curious," answers back Plum Puddin'. Inside, Plum Puddin' was afraid that Jim-Buck or Deerlores or the Granddeer might have revealed his Magical Secret with Santa, but they hadn't. And he was relieved!

CHAPTER 14: THREE YEARS LATER ON DECEMBER 23

Purple Mouse was now getting older and Maroon was finding it harder, and harder to keep his magical Christmas Secret about Santa and Plum Puddin' from Purple Mouse. So Maroon would ask him to go out in the forest and cut down a Christmas tree for the cabin and also cut another one for his room upstairs. Purple Mouse loved having his own room and loved it at Christmas time when he could have his own tree. He had a lot of special things that Plum Puddin' and many of his friends had given him. Plum Puddin' was a writer of songs and stories and Purple Mouse got a kick out of reading and hearing them. Plum Puddin' even wrote stories about Purple Mouse and Snowdeer and their adventures in the forest. Maroon and Orchid told Purple Mouse that before he was born, Terrie Young Deer had given him the special name, Lucky Clover. So, Purple Mouse had started collecting 4-leaf clovers. He had Indian skins hanging on his walls that Taneycomo and Meramec had skinned just for him. Terrie Young Deer and Niangua made sure that Horn of Plenty's fruits, nuts, and vegetables were always in plentiful supply. Ken-Buck and Mark-Buck would come by at Christmas time and bring him Pine Cone Chips. Todd Lott would come by with Glister and would let Purple Mouse take the wagon over to Knob Lick to get supplies for the family and do Christmas shopping. Harley had, by now become great friends with Purple Mouse and the family and he would drop by and bring nuts he had picked and then sing for him and the family. So, all in all Purple Mouse was blessed with a wonderful life. One of his favorite things he enjoyed was having his own set of stairs that led up to the ceiling in his bedroom that had a special door that opened to the roof. He would lie outside on that roof for hours and look at the clouds during the day and the stars at night. He also lay on the roof for years on Christmas Eve hoping to see Santa and his reindeer. But by the time Santa would come, Purple Mouse had already gone to bed and had missed his coming.

Now every December 23rd, Plum Puddin' would take his magical diamond studded jar filled with Plum Pudding and head off to the North Pole without Purple Mouse ever knowing. But this year, when they sent Purple Mouse to go cut down Christmas trees so Plum Puddin' could secretly take off, well, he found the trees sooner than normal and brought them back and left them outside so he could come in the cabin and get some water. And when he came in the back door that was in the corner of the room, he looked over at the hearth and saw Plum Puddin' and Pinecone. The cabin was filled with the smell of Plum Pudding because Plum Puddin' had just made a fresh batch. He was holding the brightly beaming diamond studded jar that was filled with Plum

Pudding and as Purple Mouse watched in amazement, Plum Puddin' said to Pinecone, "Are you ready, Pinecone?" Purple Mouse saw Pinecone jump and bark and put his paws on Plum Puddin's knees. Then he heard Plum Puddin' say the magic words Santa gave him. "HO, HO, HO, OFF TO THE NORTH POLE WE GO!" All of a sudden Plum Puddin' and Pinecone disappeared! Purple Mouse sat there confused, and surprised that Plum Puddin' had never told him that he could do that!

Purple Mouse slowly brought in the Christmas trees and laid Plum Puddin's tree by the hearth. Then dragged his own tree upstairs and laid down on his bed and fell fast asleep. In his dreams he kept seeing Plum Puddin' disappear and when he awoke he decided he would ask his parents what was going on and how many years had Plum Puddin' been going to the North Pole.

When his parents got back, Purple Mouse asked them if they knew about Plum Puddin's magical jar and how he and Pinecone would go to the North Pole. "Yes, we know son, said Maroon. Plum Puddin' and your mother and I agreed not to tell you because we didn't want to scare you. We were going to tell you when you got older. Please believe us." "Oh, I believe you, said Purple Mouse. It was just confusing to see it happen and not know he could do it." "Well, when he gets back we will have a nice talk about his travels to see Santa, Mrs. Santa, the Elves, and the Reindeer," said Maroon. "Wow, he can really see all of that?" Purple Mouse asks, his excitement growing. "Yes, he can see all of that, and your father and I are glad you know about it now. And to be honest, we'd like to go there ourselves someday." laughs Orchid. Purple Mouse, now completely comfortable knowing Plum Puddin's secret says, "I want to go too! You know Mom and Daddy, for Christmas this year, I want a magical jar like Plum Puddin's so I can go see Santa too!" "That sounds like a great idea." says Maroon and then he adds, "I hear that if you didn't get your Christmas Wish List to Santa early, then all you have to do is write down what you want and put that Wish List on the roof and somehow he magically sees it and can answer your late request." "That great!" Says Purple Mouse. "Let's put our wishes together on the same paper and I'll run it up on the roof!"

CHAPTER 15: CHRISTMAS EVE WITH THE MOUSES AND PLUM PUDDIN'S FAMILY

Later that night, Purple Mouse is still excited about having written his Christmas Wish Letter to Santa. He's lying in bed finding it hard to sleep and wondering how Santa can see a late Christmas Wish List all the way from the North Pole. He finally decides not to worry about it and drifts off to sleep.

The next morning, Christmas Eve, Maroon, Orchid and Purple Mouse wake up excited and rush downstairs to see if Plum Puddin' has made it back yet. When they don't see him, they call for Pinecone but he doesn't answer either. Then they go outside to check the shed, the barn, the chicken house and the turkey house, with no sign of Plum Puddin' or Pinecone. After a long time of calling and looking, they finally decide that they have stayed longer at the North Pole this year and that maybe they are helping Santa get ready for his Christmas flight.

They go ahead and prepare for Plum Puddin's relatives to come for Christmas Eve, just like they have for many years. Darrell and Rose Marie come over from Knob Lick and Plum Puddin's Grandparents Charles and Freda Carron come over from Bloomsdale. For years, it's been a family tradition that they fix the meal on Christmas

Eve at Plum Puddin's cabin. Even though Plum Puddin' wasn't there this Christmas Eve, they decided to cook there anyway. Rose Marie always fixes Chicken and Dumplin's. Grandma Freda always fixes Liver Dumplin's and Grandpa Charles always brings whatever vegetable he has picked from his garden patch. They always have Plum Pudding for Plum Puddin', but this year he's not here. Rose Marie and Grandma Freda go ahead and make it anyway.

While the ladies are making the meal, Grandpa Charles, Darrell, Maroon and Purple Mouse put up the tree in the front window of the cabin. They find the boxes of decorations that Plum Puddin' had upstairs along with the sleigh and reindeer that Grandma and Grandpa Carron had made. They bring it all downstais. By the time they get the tree up and all the decorations hung, Rose Marie and Grandma Freda have the dumplings made with all of the trimmings. They sit at the big wooden table with the checkered table cloth, thank the Lord for their food and then dig into their Christmas Eve meal. They have a wonderful time visiting and catching up on what has been going on in each other's families. Grandma and Grandpa Carron have seven kids and they talk about each of them and their Grand and Great Grandchildren. Maroon and Orchid talk about their move from Mouse Trap to their home there at Plum Puddin's cabin and how thankful they are to have such a great place to live with great friends. They also talk about how much fun Plum Puddin' and Pinecone must be having at the North Pole getting to see Santa, Mrs. Santa, and all the elves, but they joked that he missed out on a good meal at the cabin with them!

After supper, Purple Mouse says, "Let's sing some Christmas Carols! I'll go get Plum Puddin's guitar and we'll sing around the tree." So he goes to Plum Puddin's bedroom and gets Plums guitar that his Daddy Darrell and Mama Rose Marie got for him when he was six years old. They begin singing, Hark, The Herald Angels Sing, Joy to the World, Silent Night, and O Holy Night. Then Purple Mouse remembers that Plum Puddin' has some songs he has written that are in a cigar box and he goes and digs them out. They begin singing, Ozark Country Christmas, That Wonderful Christmas Time of Year, Jesus Christ Born the King of Kings, What Christmas Means to Me, Wise Men Still Seek Him Today and a few others Plum Puddin' had written. Then Grandpa Charles says, "Hey, let's go out and carol to the neighbors and at Holy Moly's Church! They have their Christmas Eve Service tonight!" So outside they go and walk over to Holy Moly and his wife's church, the Knob Lick Church on Molehill. They see Vivian, the church member who was in the outhouse when it got tipped over-along with her husband Roy. They also see Terrie Young Deer,

Niangua, Taneycomo, Meramec, Todd Lot and his family and even Tongue-Tied and Moss the frog brothers! They all sing until they're hoarse and finally Grandpa Charles says, "Let's call it a night and head back home before it gets too late. I want to be at home and in bed before Santa comes! I don't want to miss out on my present!" They all laugh with him and then start heading home.

CHAPTER 16: MAROON, ORCHID AND PURPLE MOUSE'S PLANS TO SEE SANTA

Later that night, when all have gone home, Purple Mouse, Orchid and Maroon sit around the Christmas tree and talk of past Christmases when they went caroling and spending time with Plum Puddin' and his family. They laugh how Purple Mouse found out firsthand about Plum Puddin' and his special secret with Santa. Oh, how great it must be up at the North Pole with all of the Elves and Reindeer and how busy it must be this time of year!

"I guess Santa will be takin' off before long" says Purple Mouse. "He has a big world to deliver presents to and I bet he has to leave early to get it all done. How I would love to go with him on his travels and see his village up there." "Yes, that would be great" says Orchid. "I know I've wanted to see it for myself but the chances of that are like a man being able to fly to the moon!" she laughs.

"Hey, speaking of Santa and flying, you did leave our Christmas Wish List for Santa on the roof, right Purple Mouse?" asks Orchid. "Yes Ma'am, I sure did." says an excited Purple Mouse. "Well," Orchid continues, "I got a fun idea. Why don't we go hide ourselves in the barn and keep watching the cabin to see Santa when he and his

Reindeer fly in tonight and see Him go down the chimney. Then we can see what He does with the Christmas Wish List!" "Great idea," says Maroon. Then Purple Mouse says, "I got an idea too. Why don't we take our presents for each other out to the barn and do our gift exchange out there while we're watching for Santa?" "Ha Ha Purple Mouse. Any excuse to open presents early," laughs Orchid. "Well, wha' do ya think," asks Purple Mouse. "Yes, let's do it son," says Maroon. Orchid gives a stern look at both Purple Mouse and Maroon and then breaks out laughing and says, "Just Kidding, I'd love to do that too!" They all laugh and Orchid continues. "Y'all go get those presents and I'll bring out some pecan pie and lemon meringue pie that I made for Christmas dinner. We'll have some pie for tomorrow too. That is, if there's any left boys!" laughs Orchid. Maroon and Purple Mouse look at each other and shrug their shoulders and Maroon laughs and says, "I'm not gonna make any promises that there will be any for tomorrow! OK, let's head to the barn and get ready for Santa!"

CHAPTER 17: CHRISTMAS EVE IN THE BARN

So, Maroon, Orchid, and Purple Mouse light lanterns and take pies and gifts to the barn. They push hay bales together and put a checkered table cloth on top of them to put everything on. Then Orchid says, "I'm gonna go back to the cabin. I forgot something." So, she leaves and in a few minutes returns with another pie and three Christmas stockings. One stocking is green, one is red and another one is purple, each with names on the front. "Hum... What you got there?" asks Maroon. "I had an apple pie that I had prepared for Christmas Dinner and decided to bring it over here," says Orchid. "What's in the Christmas stockings?" Purple Mouse asks as he picks up his purple stocking with his name on it. "It's filled with goodies, but there's something special in there you're gonna love," says Orchid. As Purple Mouse and Maroon reach into their stockings they discover the surprise hidden in the bottom, and together, they holler, "CHEESE!" "It doesn't get any better than this!" says Purple Mouse. So, they go through their stockings bringing out everything and admiring the treasures Orchid has given them. They both give Orchid a kiss on each cheek at the same time and purple Mouse asks Orchid, "Mom, would you slice the apple pie please and I'll slice some of the cheese you gave me. I've been so hungry for cheese that I could eat it and apple pie together!" So, to this day, the world still eats apple pie with cheese on top!

    After they have eaten till they could eat no more, Maroon looks at his pocket watch and says, "Let's open Christmas gifts and after that we can start looking for Santa!" "What an exciting night," says Orchid. "What else could happen that could be any better than this?" "Yes, God is so good," says Maroon. So they bow their heads and give a prayer of thanks. They had barely said Amen when Purple Mouse says, "I'll play Santa and pass out the presents!" So, Purple Mouse puts on a Santa cap and passes out gifts and they laugh and enjoy their time together as a family. The first gift Purple Mouse gives his parents is a hand carved wooden piece of his Mom and Dad that he carved with some help from Plum Puddin' and his uncle Wild Plum. He also carved salt and pepper shakers for them and a cheese cutting block. His next gift to them is a wooden churn to churn milk from some of Plum Puddin's cows so they would have fresh butter. "Purple Mouse, you have outdone yourself and we thank you," says Maroon. "We couldn't have had a better son than you," says Orchid. They hug and then Maroon says, "It's time to give you your present Purple Mouse. It's hidden here in the barn over in that corner." So, Purple Mouse grabs a lantern and goes over to the dark corner and finds a big patchwork quilt covering something pretty good sized. As he uncovers the surprise, his jaw drops. "A wagon!" he shouts. "Yes, Purple Mouse, a wagon," says Maroon. "Now you're at the age that you should have your own and be able to take your friends riding and go to the Knob Lick Store to get supplies. Wow, a wagon! Thank you very much!" says Purple Mouse. Then Orchid says, "You might want to check out the corral outside behind the barn." Purple Mouse grabs a lantern and rushes outside. In the distance, he can barely see that there's something at the other end of the big corral. By the light of the full moon he can make out that it is an animal. "What is it?" asks Purple Mouse. "Well, ya gotta have a horse to pull your wagon, don't ya?" asks Maroon laughing. "Whoa!" says, Purple Mouse as he starts walking across the big corral toward his new horse leaving his parents behind so he can enjoy time with his new present. As he gets closer, his lantern light shows a beautiful black mare. "I'm gonna call her Charcoal," says Purple Mouse as he reaches out to pet her. Charcoal grunts a little letting Purple Mouse know she likes him. "Got her from uncle Wild Plum," says Maroon. "What a Christmas this is," says Purple Mouse as he mounts Charcoal and rides around the corral. "I think the two of them are gonna get along just fine" says Orchid. "Yes, what a great companion for Him," says Maroon.

Purple Mouse tightly holds Charcoal's mane because he doesn't have a saddle on her.

Then he puts his heels into her side and hollers, "Giddy Up!" Then Purple Mouse hears a voice saying, "Hey don't kick so hard! I've got a baby in there!" Purple Mouse looks around wondering where that voice came from when Charcoal speaks again and says, "Hello Purple Mouse. Yes, I do talk! Now don't fall off!" And then she starts laughing with a loud and hearty whinny. Purple Mouse jumps off and walks to the front of her holding his lantern and bringing it up close to her face so he can look right into her eyes. This just makes Charcoal whinny and laugh more and Purple Mouse says, "You do speak!" "Yes, I sure do," answers Charcoal. Uncle Wild Plum had me for several years and your folks traded firewood and crops so you could have me in time for Christmas! Your Mother made quilts of patchwork and cross stitch – lots of them – so I could be yours. So, here I am! Now the family is going to get even bigger because we are going to have a colt." "We?" asks Purple Mouse. "Yes, replied Charcoal. Your folks don't know it yet but Uncle Wild Plum and Auntie Blossom couldn't stand for us to be separated and especially with me going to have a new one so they have given my husband Brownback to your parents! Now you will have us both to pull your wagon and when it's time to have the little one, Brownback will still be there to pull it for you." "That is wonderful" says Purple Mouse. "Let's go tell them! Are you gonna tell them you talk?" asks Purple Mouse. "Yes, we might as well tell them everything," laughs Charcoal. "They aren't gonna believe this." says Purple Mouse. "Sure they will." replies Charcoal. "But first I want you to meet Brownback." So, they leave through the back of the corral and find Brownback standing in the trees hidden out of sight. He had been watching his wife and unborn colt with a careful eye to see how Purple Mouse would react to his new gift. As they reach Brownback, Charcoal introduces Purple Mouse and Purple Mouse says, "How do you do Mr. Brownback. Do you talk too sir?" "Yes, I do," answers Brownback. "Wow" says Purple Mouse. "What a pleasure to meet you all! My folks are going to be so excited! Let's go and I'll introduce you to them!"

As Purple Mouse, Charcoal and Brownback are walking toward Maroon and Orchid, they hear Maroon holler, "Are you alright?" "Yes, we are Mr. Mouse," says Brownback. "What? Who is that?" asks Maroon. "It's me with a couple of friends," says Purple Mouse. "Huh?" says Orchid. As they get closer, the Mouses see Brownback and stand there puzzled. "Mom and Daddy, this is Brownback, Charcoal's husband. Uncle Wild Plum has given him to you because he didn't want to see them separated. Also, Charcoal is going to have a little colt! So, let me introduce you to them." As Purple Mouse makes the introductions, they answer back Hello and Maroon about drops his lantern while Orchid starts running toward the barn! "Stop!" shouts Purple Mouse. "God has blessed them with the ability to speak. Plus, they are family now. We will have many fun times and make lots of memories! And we will all be together when the new one is born." Maroon and Orchid settle down and then start talking with Brownback and Charcoal and then invite them into the barn.

"Here's the wagon we got Purple Mouse for Christmas," said Maroon. "We're gonna get a lot of use out of it." laughs Brownback. "I enjoy pullin' wagons. It sure beats working out in the fields like the mules do." he laughs. "I agree," says Charcoal. Then Orchid says, "We were having a gift exchange and eating pie out here in the barn. I don't know if you eat pie but you are sure welcome to some, or to some hay." "Apple pie for me," says Charcoal. Brownback says, "Hay for me." They are spending time getting to know each other when Maroon says, "We are planning to watch for Santa to come here tonight. We left a Christmas Wish Letter on top of the cabin and we are going to see if he gets it. Wanna join us in watching for Santa?" "Yes, we would love to." says Charcoal. So they all take their places right inside the barn doors watching for Santa and his Reindeer to arrive.

CHAPTER 18: SANTA'S ARRIVAL AT THE CABIN

They watched for hours and finally couldn't stay awake anymore and drifted off to sleep. But no sooner had they fallen asleep when they awakened by bells jingling and a deep voice ringing through the forest with a thunderous, but joyful "HO-HO-HO!". They sneaked out of the barn and hid under a big hickory tree where they thought Santa wouldn't see them. They watched as he landed on the cabin roof. There was a special magical snow that was flying around the reindeer causing Purple Mouse and the whole gang to stare in wonder. They watched Santa get out of his sleigh and pet each reindeer before going over to pick up Purple Mouse, Orchid, and Maroon's Christmas Wish Letter. He reads it, belly laughs another "HO-HO-HO" and goes over to the sleigh to get his big magical bag. Santa grabs the sack and goes over to the chimney. After placing both feet inside, and sitting on the edge of it, he puts his toy bag on his back and hops down. The bag was too big to naturally go down the chimney but with Santa's magic, it fits perfectly. The thrill of seeing Santa is broken when in the distance they hear a mountain lion's roar. They all see the lion at the same time. He sees them and starts running toward them. Charcoal runs to the barn and Brownback puts his back to the mountain lion and starts kicking at it while hollering at the Mouses to run for the cabin. Orchid, Maroon and Purple Mouse make a mad dash for it and while Brownback is distracting the mountain lion. They reach the steps at the side of the cabin that go up to the roof and climb to safety. They are thankful that Purple Mouse had built those steps as a way of going up to the roof entrance to his room upstairs.

Brownback looks up and sees that the Mouses are safe, so he bends forward and gives one last kick at the mountain lion. Brownback's hoof lands squarely in the mountain lion's face, dazing him and sending him running off into the woods. Brownback rushes into the barn to check on Charcoal and finds her doing great. Purple Mouse and his folks had gotten onto the roof safely, but no sooner had they gotten there, than they hear Santa coming up the chimney! In a panic, not wanting Santa to see them, Orchid and Maroon run and hide behind the back seat in the sleigh where Santa keeps his magical sack. Purple Mouse doesn't have enough time to follow them so he rushes over to his roof door that leads to his living quarters and climbs in. He makes it just in time and closes the door as he hears Santa say to his Reindeer, "HO-HO-HO! LET'S HEAD TO THE NORTH POLE!" Then Purple Mouse opens his door in time to see Santa take off to the North Pole with Orchid and Maroon hanging onto the back of Santa's sleigh. Purple Mouse hollers "Mom, Daddy!" as they trail off in the distance, sadly looking back and waving frantically at him.

CHAPTER 19: WHAT'LL I DO NOW?

Purple Mouse stands on the roof of the cabin watching his folks and Santa until they fly completely out of sight. Then he looks up into the heavens into the bright starry Christmas sky and says, "God, What'll I do now? Will they ever come back or will I have to go to....Wait!" He says out loud. "Yes! I'll get to them. But how?" Then he remembers he had asked Santa for a magical jar so he could go to the North Pole. Purple Mouse quickly goes down through his roof hideaway and dashes downstairs to find the beautiful diamond studded jar with the purple lid and a big "S" on it by the fireplace. Overjoyed, Purple Mouse says a big, "Thank You Lord," and rushes to see if Plum Puddin's mother Rose Marie has left any Plum Pudding from their Christmas Eve get together. Thankfully she had left some, so Purple Mouse grabs a wooden spoon from the cupboard drawer and starts filling the magical jar. As he puts the first dip of Plum Puddin' in, he notices the jar starting to light up. This startled him so much that he fumbles the jar and almost drops it! But as he once again gets a solid grip on the jar and finishes filling it with Plum Pudding, it becomes fully lit and beautiful. After he puts the last drop of Plum Pudding in, he licks the spoon and tightens the purple lid. He knows exactly what to do because he had heard Plum Puddin' say the magic words before. So, Purple Mouse holds the magical jar in his right hand and says, "HO-HO-HO! OFF TO THE NORTH POLE WE GO!" He starts feeling tingly and then a big flash of light goes around him and he disappears from the cabin! Purple Mouse didn't know it, but Charcoal and Brownback had been watchin' from outside the cabin window. They both reared up and whinnied at the sight of the flash of light and Purple Mouse's disappearance! They look at each other and Brownback says, "Charcoal, are we sure we want to be in this family?" Charcoal laughs and says, "You bet! And I can tell you already that we'll never ever have a day of boredom!" Brownback wholeheartedly agrees and says, "Well, let's get back to the barn. It's cold tonight and the night air is makin' me a little... "HORSE!" he jokes. "Very funny." says Charcoal. "But, I'm sorry. I have to correct you my dear. I'm the one who is making you a little HORSE!" They both laugh and head back to the barn to enjoy the rest of their Christmas Eve together in their new home.

CHAPTER 20: FLYIN' THROUGH THE CHRISTMAS SKY WITH SANTA

Meanwhile, way above Charcoal and Brownback, flying through the night is Santa; his team of deer and two frightened mice hanging on for dear life on the back of Santa's sleigh. All of a sudden a big wind of snow swirls behind them and blows them up and over into the sleigh. The wind is so powerful that Santa almost looses the reins to the deer! He seems not to have noticed that Orchid and Maroon were in the back seat! The padding in his sleigh is so thick that it doesn't hurt them at all. Not wanting to upset Santa or the deer, they both quickly jump into Santa's magical bag that is empty because Plum Puddin's cabin was Santa's last stop. Once inside, they hold the edges of the sack over their heads with only their faces peeking out and watch Santa and the deer fly upward back to the North Pole.

Once they hopped in Santa's magical sack, the magic inside it made Maroon and Orchid's fear melt away. They look at each other and start to grin. They begin to giggle like school children but quickly cover their mouths because they don't want Santa to hear them. They're enchanted with the beautiful Christmas sky and the feeling of knowing they are safe with Santa! But then a thought hits Orchid and she asks, "Dear, do you think Santa granted Purple Mouse's wish to receive his own magical jar?" "Yes, I really do believe he did and I bet we'll see him during our time at the North Pole if Santa has anything to do with it!," Maroon laughs. Then Orchid says, "I sure hope so. I couldn't stand to leave our son in the cabin without us on Christmas. We've never missed a Christmas together since he has been born." "Yes, I know, says Maroon, and Lord willin' we'll be together again for this Christmas too!"

CHAPTER 21: DOESN'T THAT LOOK LIKE SNOWDEER?

"What's that powdery lookin' stuff that's surrounding the deer?" Maroon asks. "I don't know. Santa's back is blocking me from seeing the deer very well," answers Orchid. Then she stands up and looks around Santa and sees the snowy haze around each deer. It swirls around them and then shoots up into the sky for a while and then comes back and swirls around the deer again. She is mesmerized by it and says, "It's so beautiful and magical!" Then she realizes and says to Maroon, "That's what blew us up and over into the sleigh! I believe that that snow is what Santa uses to make his deer fly! You know. I think we may have learned another little secret about Santa. Between his secret with Plum Puddin' and this magical snow around his deer, Santa has surprises that I ever imagined! And wait! Speaking of surprises, doesn't that look like Snowdeer in front pulling Santa's sleigh?" asks Maroon. "You know, it does look like him. Snowdeer is the only solid white deer I have ever known. That's got to be him!" says Orchid. "Well, when we get to the North Pole, we'll find out for sure." says Maroon. "And since we are talking about the North Pole, remember; Santa doesn't know we're here, so when we get there we'd better stay in his magical sack and hide until we can talk to him by ourselves."

"That sounds great to me." says Orchid.

"We'll talk to him while he's putting his sleigh back in the sleigh barn."

CHAPTER 22: MAROON AND ORCHID MEET JOSH ELF

By the time they arrived at the North Pole, Maroon and Orchid had fallen into a deep sleep inside Santa's magical toy bag. They didn't have the magical snow on them that Santa puts on the deer and himself, so they tired out and didn't last through the trip. And to make things worse, the magical bag tied itself back up with them in it and they couldn't get out! So, when Maroon and Orchid woke up from their deep sleep, they realized that not only were they trapped in the magical sack, but they had also missed the Welcome Home celebration. Being trapped in Santa's magical bag meant that they didn't get to see Santa, so they could talk with him!

At this point, Maroon and Orchid don't know where they are, but they figure they're probably in Santa's sleigh barn and they don't know how long it might be before anyone will come in and find them! So they start hollering out, "HELP! HELP! Is anyone here?" All is quiet and they start hollering it again. Finally they hear keys rattling and a key unlocking a door. Then they hear the squeaking sound of a door opening and the voice of an elf singing, "Joy to the World, the Lord is come!" Maroon and Orchid shout out again, "HELP! HELP!" and a very surprised elf stops singing and looks around to see where the voices are coming from. "Where are you?" the elf asks.

"We're here in Santa's magical sack," they answer. "Huh?" asks the elf. "We're over here in Santa's toy bag. Please get us out. The bag is tied and we can't untie it" they say. "Oh, there you are," says the elf and he goes over and unties the bag to let them out. "Thank you very much, Mr. Elf" they say and the elf replies, "You're welcome. Please call me Josh. I'm Santa's Official singing elf. Santa has asked me to go around the North Pole Village and sing to all who live here. I make recordings and I'm played on the North Pole's Radio Station CMAS all the time! JB the DJ Elf and I do interviews and we do our annual Christmas Elf Fest here at First Elfbyterian Church. My parents Dale and Melody Elf have MelodyDale's Music Store if you ever need anything musical." "Thanks a lot Josh, we sure do appreciate your kindness," says Maroon. "How did you get here?" asks Josh. "Well, it's a long story." says Maroon. "We live with our son Purple Mouse down in Possum Holler by Knob Lick located in the Ozarks in the United States. We live upstairs in our friend Plum Puddin's cabin." "Plum Puddin'?" asks Josh. "I know him well! He comes up here every Christmas with his dog Pinecone and brings Santa and Mrs. Santa a jar of Plum Pudding." "Yes, that's him." says Maroon. "He has become family to us and when we didn't have a place to stay, he took us in. When our son Purple Mouse was born, he did everything he could to make us feel at home. Plum Puddin' told us his special secret about the Magical Jar and the magic words that would take him here to the North Pole. We were so excited but we kept the secret from Purple Mouse for a long time. Well, the other day Purple Mouse caught Plum Puddin' as he was saying the magic words and saw him disappear! He was amazed by it, but also shocked that no one had ever told him about this secret. He came to us and we had to tell him that we knew about it but didn't keep it from him to be mean; we just wanted to wait till the right time. So, I guess when he caught Plum Puddin' disappearing, it was the right time!" They all laugh and Maroon continues, "Purple Mouse wanted to ask Santa for a Magical Jar too, so he wrote a special Christmas Wish Letter to Santa and left it on the roof so Santa could find it easily and read it. Then later, we went out to our barn to exchange gifts and watch for Santa to come. We did see Santa arrive but then a mountain lion came out of nowhere and we ran for our lives to the roof of our cabin. As we got on the roof, we heard Santa coming back up the chimney and we had to hurry and hide so he wouldn't see us. We decided the only place we had to hide was hanging on the back of Santa's sleigh behind Santa's magical sack. Purple Mouse didn't have time to hide with us, so he quickly went down his roof entrance to hide from Santa. Santa didn't see us and we had to stay hidden. But then, Santa took off suddenly and we had to hold on to his sleigh because it took off so fasts The last time we saw

Purple Mouse was when we looked back and heard him hollering, "Mom-Daddy." All we could do was wave goodbye. Our hope is that Santa brought him the Magical Jar he wanted. Then, he could be here at the North Pole for Christmas celebrate with us, Santa, Mrs. Santa and the whole North Pole gang!"

"Well, we'll see about that, says Josh. I'll be making my rounds after our Christmas meal and I'll look for him tonight at Santa's Annual Christmas Party Square Dance. Well, actually it's all kinds of music and not just square dance music. My mom, Melody, sings and plays fiddle and my dad, Dale, sings and plays guitar in it! I sing and play guitar in it too. Would you like to join me, Amber and Lilly Kay for Christmas supper and then we can all head over to Elf Hall for the Christmas Party Dance? There will be Santa's famous eggnog, wassail and hot cocoa along with finger foods and all the candy canes and chocolate candy you can eat!" "Oh yes, we would be honored to be your guests," Orchid replies. "Great! Let's get you both out of Santa's Magical Sack and head over to our cottage for Christmas supper!

As they leave Santa's sleigh barn they run into Harvey the reindeer preparation elf and Josh says, "Harvey! Great to see you! Wanna meet my friends?" "Yes," answers Harvey. "Ok, this is

Maroon and Orchid Mouse and they came here on Santa's sleigh," says Josh. "Well, Welcome! HA-HA-HA-HO-HO-HO!" says Harvey. "I'm Harvey the reindeer preparation elf. I work in Santa's Reindeer Barn taking care of Santa's reindeer all year long. Then when Christmas Eve arrives, I make sure they are all ready to pull Santa's sleigh to deliver presents to all the boys and girls and animals in the whole world!"

"Wow, that's a big task!" says Orchid.

"Yes ma'am it is, says Harvey. And this year I really messed up. I got into Santa's magical snow called, Sugar Snow. It's only supposed to be used on Santa's reindeer. It not only makes them fly; they never tire out so they can keep going all Christmas Eve night. Well, I got into it and put a little bit on my toes so I'd feel good and tingly but a little Sugar Snow goes a long way! HA-HA-HA-HO-HO-HO! I started flyin' and ping ponging from one end of the reindeer barn to the other and couldn't come down! I'd left the water hose running while filling the reindeer water troughs and left it on for hours 'cause I couldn't get down to turn it off! This happened while the reindeer were asleep. They lay in the water for hours and woke up sick with colds and couldn't pull Santa's sleigh this year! I felt terrible but they forgave me. And thank the Lord, a special little solid white buck, by the name of Snowdeer had a special

Christmas wish. He wanted to pull Santa's sleigh! And because the reindeer were sick, Santa granted his wish."

"Snowdeer? We know him!" say Orchid and Maroon together. "He's our neighbor down at Doe Run in the Ozarks!"

"Well, HA-HA-HA-HO-HO-HO!" says Harvey. "He and his family are here right now! Hey, do you by any chance know Plum Puddin'?" "Do we know him?" says Maroon. "We not only know him, we live with him in his cabin!" "He's up here right now along with his Mama Rose Marie and his Daddy Darrell," says Harvey. Then Josh says, "That's great Harvey! Thank you for letting us know about him and the others. Well, let's go have supper at my cottage with Amber and Lilly Kay and then head over to Santa's Christmas Party tonight. We'll look for you and for Plum Puddin' and his folks when we're there," says Josh. "That sounds great," says Harvey. "Are they gonna be surprised to see you! Well, I'm off to check the reindeer. Gonna get them spiffed up for the party tonight! They're gonna do a special dance with Snowdeer tonight called, The Happy Hoof Dance! HA-HA-HA-HO-HO-HO! OFF TO THE REINDEER BARN I GO!" And as always, he's in a hurry and zips off for the Reindeer Barn to get the reindeer ready.

As they arrive at Josh Elf's cabin, he opens the door and sticks his head in and says, "Honey Elf, we have company!" "Great! Have them come in," answers Josh Elf's wife, Amber Elf. She's a beautiful elf and loves having company. She's also a teacher for the young elves at the North Pole Elementary School. They have a beautiful young elf of their own by the name of Lilly Kay Elf. Then Josh says, "Amber, this is Maroon and Orchid Mouse." "Nice to meet you." she replies. "I'm Amber Elf and that is Lilly Kay Elf." She points over toward their Christmas tree and they see a young elf singing while hanging decorations on it. "We had Christmas ornament exchange this week at school and a lot of new ornaments were brought home!" laughs Amber Elf. "I invited Maroon and Orchid for Christmas supper," says Josh. "We would love to have you stay and eat," says Amber Elf. "Do you need any help getting ready?" offers Orchid. "Yes please," answers Amber and off they go to the kitchen. Josh and Maroon watch little Lilly Kay humming and decorating their beautiful tree. Then Josh says, "You know, I forgot to tell Harvey about Purple Mouse. I wonder if he has seen him." "Well, we will definitely find out tonight Josh." says Maroon. "We miss him terribly. We've never had a Christmas without him. What a special blessing it would be if he were here." Then Maroon perks up and says, "Speaking of a special blessing, here comes Christmas supper!" They watch as Amber and Orchid pop out of the kitchen with a big Christmas feed! Then Josh goes over to the Christmas tree and picks up little Lilly Kay and they join around the tiny elf sized table, all decorated for Christmas. Maroon offers a prayer of blessing for the food, and also asks the Lord to help them find Purple Mouse. Then they start digging into the wonderful Christmas meal.

CHAPTER 23: A WHOLE LOT OF MEWS

They didn't know it, but Purple Mouse had definitely arrived at the North Pole. He was magically taken there, just like Plum Puddin' had been many times before. But in Purple Mouse's case, instead of going right down to Santa's Village, he had fallen into a deep sleep on the other side of North Pole Mountain right behind the North Pole Marker and had been there for hours. The Sugar Snow that Santa uses on his reindeer is always falling at the North Pole's Pole and Santa keeps some of it in his special trunk in the Reindeer Barn. Each flake of Sugar Snow has its own personality. Some are super friendly, some are mischievous, some are smiley, and some like to blow cold air on you as they fly by. And all of the flakes have the ability to take on a magical illumination or turn different colors. Well, some of them decide to wake up Purple Mouse. They start blowing cold air on him and landing on top of him and some other flakes tickle his nose and ears. The coldness along with the sounds of them laughing and tickling him make Purple Mouse wake up. As he opens his eyes and yawns and stretches, he hears Christmas music coming from a radio station that has a big tall tower with a sign on it with the call letters, CMAS. He rushes to the top of the North Pole Mountain and looks down the hill to see Santa's Village and immediately becomes wide awake. He watches anxiously as giggling elf children teeter totter and others slide down miles and miles of multi-colored slides. Purple Mouse then looks behind him and sees a big oversized cat that has been watching him. Purple Mouse begins to panic because he's a mouse and he's scared of cats. But just as he's getting ready to run, the cat starts laughing and hits the ground with his two front paws and makes Sugar Snow fly everywhere! He rolls around laughing in the snow and says, "Hello, my name is Hew. I'm one of Santa's special singing cats. I bet you thought this was your first *and* last day at the North Pole, didn't you?" "Yes, I did," answers Purple Mouse. Then Hew says, "There's no way I would ever hurt you. Why, if I did anything to you, Santa would put me on the Naughty List and never take me off! And that would be CAT-A-STROPHIC! Ha, ha, ha." he laughs again. "Well, at least I know I'm safe," laughs Purple Mouse and then he asks, "Are there any more cats or mice here and if there are, are they nice like you?" "Oh yes, there are more cats and mice here and they're all nice. We only have the finest of the litter! Ha, ha, ha." Hew laughs again. Then Purple Mouse says, "You are quite a joker, Hew! Oh, let me introduce myself, I'm Purple Mouse." "How did you get here?" asks Hew. "You aren't going to believe it." answers Purple Mouse. "I live with my parents and my friend Plum Puddin' and his dog Pinecone in a place called Possum Holler by Knob Lick down in the Ozarks. How this all started is,

Plum Puddin' has a special secret with Santa. He has a special magical jar that Santa gave him. Every Christmas, when he fills it with Plum Pudding and holds the jar nice and tight in his right hand and says the magic words Santa told him to say, well, then he magically comes here to the North Pole to see Santa, Mrs. Santa and the gang." "Oh yea, Plum Puddin'. I remember him! Ain't he the cat's meow!" Then he once again hits the snow with his paw and sends it flying! Then Hew continues, "I've seen him every year that he's come here! And this is one Christmas I'll never forget. Plum Puddin', Pinecone and Santa left earlier than normal to get Snowdeer and his family in Doe Run to fly his sleigh. Then, the four of them went flying around the world together, delivering Christmas presents to all who were not on the Naughty List." "You mean Plum Puddin' and Pinecone were in the sleigh last night? Asks Purple Mouse. We never did see them." Then Hew says, "I bet that was because Santa has an extra seat in the front of him that sits lower and when Santa is driving his sleigh, you couldn't see them." "Ok, that explains that." says Purple Mouse. "And wow! Snowdeer and his family were pulling the sleigh!" "Yes, they sure did." says Hew. "They were truly a God send and what they did will be talked about for a long time." Then he asks, "Does Snowdeer and his family live near you?" "Yes, they do." answers Purple Mouse. "There's Snowdeer, his dad Jim-Buck, his mother

Deerlores, his sister Rosie, and his brothers Deerell, Antler and Longnose. Seven of them! He's also got his Uncle Ken-Buck and Uncle Mark-Buck who are his daddy Jim-Bucks brothers who have a chocolate factory in the Seymour Forest that's called, Pine Cone Chips! They're a wonderful family." "That's great! Says Hew. And speaking of family, I want you to meet the rest of my family. Our last name is Mew. My parents are Bartholomew and Deborah Lew, my brothers are Pugh, Cue, Rue, and my very cool acting brother we all call Dude Mew and a cool acting sister we call Ewe Mew! I have another sister Mewlinda that we nicknamed Mi Mew...well, actually I have a lot more brothers, and sisters but there are way too many to mention by name!" Hew laughs. "Let's go meet them," says Purple Mouse so off they go down North Pole Mountain to meet a whole lot of Mews and whoever else comes across their path.

CHAPTER 24: DUNNE'S CHRISTMAS BUNS AND STRIKE THE BELL

As Purple Mouse and Hew Mew arrive at the edge of the North Pole Village, the smell of the bakery sends them running up to the shop's window. All decorated in garland and tinsel and beautiful multi-colored lights, it looks as great as it smells! All of a sudden the shop door opens and they hear, "Merry Christmas! Welcome to Dunne's Christmas Buns Bakery!" laughs a cute little Mama elf standing there in her Christmas apron that's covered in flour. Then she continues, "My name is Judy and what can I get for you today?" she asks. "Could you bottle up this wonderful smell and sell it?" asks Purple Mouse laughing. "Ha Ha! If I could, I'd be making millions!" Judy laughs back. Then she says, "We have free samples of one of our specialties I just baked today. They're still hot and fresh. They're Cheese Rolls! Would you like to try them?" Both Purple Mouse and Hew Mew perk up and give a big Yes! And then Purple Mouse says, "I've never known a mouse to turn down an offer for cheese!" They all laugh and then Purple Mouse thanks Judy for the cheese rolls and starts telling her how he got there at the North Pole. He apologizes that he hadn't brought any money, or he would buy a dozen of them. "Oh, that's OK Purple Mouse," says Judy. "It's Christmas and I want to give you a dozen free to take with you. I wasn't open for business today anyway. I was baking all kinds of goodies to take to Santa's Christmas Party later tonight. Are you coming to the party?" "Oh, yes Ma'am, we will be there with bells on," says Purple Mouse. "That sounds great." says Judy. "Well, boys, I'm gonna get back to baking and let you look around the village. It's more magical here today than any other day of the year! Merry Christmas and enjoy your Cheese Rolls! See you at the party tonight!" And with that, she closes the shop door and Hew Mew and Purple Mouse head on to see more of the North Pole sights.

Purple Mouse and Hew Mew decide to eat some more of the Cheese Rolls while looking around but as they turn the corner they run into Henry Elf from Body by Dorn Exercise Gym. He's out on his daily run. Henry looks at them, and then at the box of rolls and says, "You'd better not eat all of those at once or I'll have to open my shop and give you a work out! Ha Ha! Just Kiddin' ya! Enjoy the rolls! That Judy makes the best bakery goods ever!" "Yes she does," they both agree. "You guys have a Merry Christmas and see you at Santa's Christmas Party tonight! Sorry, that I have to leave, but I gotta run! Get it? Gotta run?" They all burst out laughing and Purple Mouse and Hew Mew say, "Bye Henry! Merry Christmas to you too!"

As they continue looking around, Purple Mouse sees a bell standing in the middle of the village. With a funny look creeping across his face he says, "Hew, don't think I'm weird, but I think that bell has eyes and is watching us!"

"You aren't weird Purple Mouse, " answers Hew. "The bell's name is Strike and he rings to let everyone know when Santa is leaving to deliver gifts on Christmas Eve. He rings when Santa returns. Strike will also ring if there is any emergency too."

"That's really cool Hew'" says Purple Mouse. "Can we meet him?"

"Sure, answers Hew." and off they go to meet Strike the Bell.

When they get there, Hew says, "Merry Christmas Strike, How are you today?" Strike rings his bell back greeting him. Then Hew says, "Strike, this is Purple Mouse." "Hello Strike, says Purple Mouse, nice to meet you." Strike rings his bell greeting Purple Mouse too. Hew, thinking he is cute and having fun says, "I don't know your face Strike, but your name rings a bell!" Both Hew and Purple Mouse bend over laughing when all of a sudden they hear a laughing voice saying, "Well, it doesn't look like the cat's got your tongue Hew! Ha, ha, ha"

At hearing that, Hew and Purple Mouse just about fall over. "Strike! I never knew you could talk! What a surprise!" says Hew. Strike then says, "You and Purple Mouse are among the very few who know. Santa placed me here many years ago and my job is to ring for him. I usually just speak to him or Mrs. Santa only because they made me keeper of the North Pole Village and I report to Santa regularly."

"This is way cool", says Purple Mouse. "It's an honor to meet you Strike."

"You too, Purple Mouse," Strike answers, and then he says, "Welcome to the North Pole Village. Come back anytime and we'll talk if no one else is around. Please keep it a secret about me being able to talk,"

"You bet! Your secret is safe with me," says Purple Mouse.

"And me too" says Hew.

As they walk off, Strike says, "Please ask Santa to make sure he has the Christmas Party music speakers pumping the music outside so I can hear it!"

They all laugh and Hew says, "Alright, I'll be sure to tell him."

CHAPTER 25: THE GOOD MEWS OF CHRISTMAS

Hew looks at Purple Mouse and says, "I've lived here at the North Pole all my life and I'm always finding out new things here!" "It's truly a magical place," says Purple Mouse. Then Hew remembers and says to Purple Mouse, "Hey, I never did introduce you to my family. I want you to hear us sing too." "Oh yea, let's do it, Hew", says Purple Mouse. "Ok, this way" says Hew. So off they head down a back road that takes them about a half a mile away to the Mew Family home. It's a huge two story home decorated with Christmas lights and assorted colored balls of yarn and cat scratchers all over the place! The fence posts in the yard are all used as scratching posts too! Their home sits at the bottom of a real tall mountain. "Welcome to Mews Mountain," says Hew to purple Mouse. As they walk up to the porch, cats scatter all over the place. Hew opens the front door and says, "Hey Everybody, I got a new friend I want you to meet! He's a mouse, but you can't eat him! Ha, ha, ha!" "Very funny Hew," says Purple Mouse. "Hope they like you Purple Mouse 'cause you're outnumbered at least 100 to 1," laughs Hew. "I sure hope so too 'cause otherwise, I'd be cat food for sure!" says Purple Mouse.

At the sounds of the laughing, cats start coming from all directions, from corners, down the stairs, and a slide that goes from the roof to the front yard. They come out from under furniture, out the mailbox, and on and on. "I've never seen such a large family in my life," says Purple Mouse. "Yes, we're the biggest family here at the North Pole and welcome friend," says a voice behind him. Purple Mouse turns around to see who said that and the voice speaks again and says, "Hello, I'm Bartholomew. Hew's father. And this is my wife Deborah Lew, Hew's mother. There's so many of us here that it would take forever to remember what everyone's name is to try introduce them to you!" laughs Bartholomew. "Hello Gang, says Purple Mouse. Nice to meet you. Please don't eat me!" And at that, they all start laughing and rolling around and telling him that they'd never do that and that Santa would put them on the Naughty List and that it would be, Cat-A-Strophic. Purple Mouse looks at Hew and says, "Wow, where have I heard that before? Your names rhyme and y'all even say the same things! Ha Ha!" "Runs in the family, my dear mouse," shoots back Hew and they both laugh as the others join in.

"Did you tell Purple Mouse that our family sings?" asks Deborah Lew. "Yes Ma'am, I did," answers Hew. "Would you like to hear us do a song?" asks Deborah Lew. "We sing at the North Pole Cathedral and we go as, The North Polecat Family Singers and I lead the Prayer Meetings at the, Cat-Thedral!" laughs Deborah Lew. They all get down laughing and as they start to settle down someone else says, "She's also Church Comedian, you may have noticed", chimes in Kevin Kilmewey-one of the neighbors who works at CMAS Radio Station. They start laughing again, and then as they finally settle completely down, Deborah Lew says, "Let's do the song we're gonna sing tonight at Santa's Annual Christmas Party" "Yes, we like that one! Let's do it!" The family says and Deborah Lew asks, "Do you all know your parts?" "Yes, we're ready", they respond. "We're gonna go in the house and prepare" says Deborah Lew. Purple Mouse takes a seat on the front porch swing and a few minutes later Deborah Lew comes out of the house and stands in the front yard and introduces the song to him. She says, "It's a song we have sung for years and has become a family tradition. It's called, The Good Mews Of Christmas!" Purple Mouse wants to laugh at the title of the song, but as he hears them start to sing as they come out the front door and around the house and down the slide into the front yard, he is enchanted by it. He also watches as some of the cats play beautiful fiddle parts and other orchestra parts. They sing it over and over until all of the Mew Family has come into the front yard or on the front porch in front of Purple Mouse. Then all of a sudden, a big wind of blowing snow coming straight from the North Pole circles around Mew Mountain and flies right by them with some snowflakes landing on them. They see happy, cheerful faces on the flakes and hear them giggling and then off they blow back to the North Pole Mountain. "They do that every year," says Deborah Lew. "And we are thankful because we know they love the song."

"If you keep this up, I'll never want to leave," laughs Purple Mouse. "We'd love for you to stay but if you couldn't, we'd want you to visit us every time you come back" says Deborah Lew. Hew and all of the family agree. "Oh my, I forgot the Jar! The Plum Pudding Jar that got me here! I left it at the North Pole Mountain and if it isn't there I'll probably be staying here forever!" laughs Purple Mouse. "I'd better get back and see if I can find it. Hew, please tell all your family the story of how I got here and I'll go hunt for my Plum Pudding Jar. Thank you all for the beautiful music. See you at the Christmas Party tonight!" Then He takes off running for the North Pole Mountain but looks back one more time to wave at them. What he sees is a big household of beautiful, talented cats, who now look, for all the world, like family, as they gaze at him and wave him on.

CHAPTER 26: CHRISTMAS CANDY CHUTES AND SANTA'S SECRET UNDERGROUND LAIR

Christmas day is quickly going by and night is beginning to fall. As Purple Mouse is heading back to the North Pole Village, he once again sees the beautiful town full of bustling elves exchanging Christmas greetings and gifts while others are skating on Peppermint Pond. Still others are just taking in the sights and sounds of the season in one of the most famous places in all the world.

All at once Purple Mouse sees a huge red chute come out of the top of Santa's Station. Then a green chute. Then a gold chute. Then a silver chute. Followed by a white chute and others. Purple Mouse runs over to check it out and watches as elves dressed in their finest elf wear roll out large barrels from the elf factory. As everything is set into place, 10 elves appear holding a huge sign written in big letters that says,

WELCOME TO SANTA'S FESTIVAL OF THE CHRISTMAS CANDY CHUTES BROUGHT TO YOU BY KRULL'S CONFECTIONARY, MARQUART'S MOLASSES AND PLUMMER'S REINDEER HARDWARE.

Then one of the elves steps up to the microphone and announces the event saying, "Welcome Everyone! I'm Chris and this is my wife Kim with our sons, Christopher and Ryan from Krull's Confectionary. We also have with us, Kellyn and Matt of Marquarts Molasses, and last, but not least we have Scott and Tina with sons Jackson and Dylan of Plummer's Reindeer Hardware. We're sponsoring tonight's event so, let the *Festival of the Christmas Candy Chutes* begin!" A great cheer comes over the crowd of elves and animals as they watch fireworks explode above them. The chutes themselves begin to light up as Christmas goodies start sliding down into the barrels for all the North Pole townsfolk. Purple Mouse watches as the chutes send forth a variety of candy canes, hard candy, chocolate bars, lemon drops, bags of chocolate covered peanuts and chocolate covered raisins. Other chutes bring forth jars of molasses, sorghum, and jams and jellies. Then out steps Santa. Purple Mouse gasps and watches Santa give a hearty "HO, HO, HO" and says, "Welcome everyone to the Candy Chute Show! Take all you want. This is all for you, with thanks from us for everything you do! Merry Christmas! HO, HO, HO!" The crowd goes wild and then Santa says, "The Christmas Party will begin at Elf Hall in one hour! Everyone is invited to this event! HO, HO, HO!" After saying that, Santa quickly leaves and the elves and the townsfolk start gathering their Christmas treasures from the chutes as they slide down. Purple Mouse stuffs his pocket with candy bars and peppermint sticks and picks up a lantern and starts to follow Santa.

Santa has moved quickly and Purple Mouse just about loses track of him. He sees Santa turn a corner at a big building and then, he's gone. Purple Mouse runs up and turns the corner and all he sees is an old building that looks like a factory that hasn't been used in years. Purple Mouse goes to one of the doors to see if Santa had gone in, but he finds it locked. Then he goes to another door and another but finds them all locked. He sits down, frustrated and begins eating on one of his chocolate bars. It's getting darker outside and all of a sudden he sees candle light coming from a little window, revealing that there is a downstairs in the building. Purple Mouse perks up again and looks over in the window. He doesn't see the candle anymore but he does see a door that is level with the ground by the building. It has Santa 777 painted on it. He gets an idea that this may be the door Santa uses that leads to a secret place that he goes to where he can be by himself. So, quickly, Purple Mouse finishes his chocolate bar and grabbing his lantern, he goes over to the door and finds it unlocked! He looks around and doesn't see anyone watching, so he quickly steps inside.

As he closes the door, he discovers there are many steps leading downward. When he gets to the bottom of the stairs, his lantern lights up a whole underground lair of toys, Christmas lists, reindeer harnesses, tools, boots, Santa suits, memorabilia and a big desk with rows and rows of books and a huge world map hanging behind it. Then, over in a corner Purple Mouse sees Santa. He has his back towards Purple Mouse and he's there working on some toys, probably for next Christmas, Purple Mouse figures. He's checking them to make sure they work and then marking them off his list, and then writing down what child they will go to. Purple Mouse could tell that Santa found great joy in giving children and animals gifts because when he would mark each toy as ready, he would give a big "HO, HO, HO" and move on to the next toy. Out of the corner of his eye, Santa has been watching Purple Mouse because he was expecting him. Purple Mouse has no idea that Santa knows he is there. He turns his back toward Santa and looks around the room, in wonder, at this magical discovery. As he turns back around, Santa is right there bent down looking at him and he says, "HO, HO, HO! What do you know! A little Purple Mouse with a lantern all aglow!" Purple Mouse almost drops his lantern and backs up in fear, having been caught. Santa sees that he's frightened and says, "Purple Mouse, don't be afraid. I've been expecting you! Welcome to Santa's secret underground lair! This is my private hideaway where I start making toys for next Christmas and invent new toys and ideas to share with the elves so they can start putting them into production! I have my own museum and my own high top chair down here where I can take long naps! HO, HO, HO! I have never ending Cocoa and all the chocolate chip cookies I can eat! And I put away a lot of them! HO, HO, HO!" he laughs again. Then he says, "Come, let's sit at my desk and talk. I want to get to know you better." So, Purple Mouse sits down and Santa brings him a big cup of hot cocoa and chocolate chip cookies and puts Purple Mouse totally at ease.

CHAPTER 27: PURPLE MOUSE MEETS TASHA

"I have another secret down here," Santa confesses. "I have my very own personal assistant. Mrs. Claus and I just love her and she has become part of our family! I'd like for you to meet her. Then he lifts his voice and says, "Tasha, would you come over here please dear?" Then from in back of the room among rows and rows of books, they see a young girl holding a candle wearing a purple dress and a hat trimmed with holly berries and ivy. As she gets closer, Purple Mouse realizes she is a mouse too! Then Santa introduces them. "Purple Mouse, please meet Tasha. Tasha, please meet Purple Mouse."

"Pleased to meet you Purple Mouse," says Tasha. Purple Mouse just stands there staring at her and begins to blush, never saying a word. But something odd starts happening. Purple Mouse's blush turns from red to purple. Something that has never happened before! Then Santa says, "Purple Mouse, as I live and breathe, You are as your name says!" "I'm what Santa?" asks Purple Mouse. "Tasha, would you get a mirror please?" asks a grinning Santa. "Yes, Santa," answers Tasha. Giggling to herself, Tasha goes and gets a mirror and hands it to Santa. As Santa holds the mirror in front of Purple Mouse's face he says, "Purple Mouse, please take a look and tell me what you see." "Yes Sir," answers Purple Mouse. As he looks at his image in the mirror he gasps and slowly moves away from it, but still starest his purple face. "Uh, what just happened?" he asks. Santa replies, "Purple Mouse, when a young man or a young elf or, in your case a young mouse meets a fine looking girl, sometimes something inside makes them blush and turn red in the face. That's what happened to you, my friend. Except in your case, you blushed in purple!" laughs Santa. "Don't be embarrassed, just ask Mrs. Claus. When I met her, my face turned as red as my suit! HO, HO, HO!"

Purple Mouse keeps looking down, still embarrassed. He suddenly realizes that he hasn't yet spoken to Tasha. He decides to try to put his shyness aside and an uneasy "Hello Tasha, it's a pleasure to meet you." escapes from his uncertain lips. And at that, he blushes again. Tasha giggles, and Purple Mouse looks at Santa and rolls his eyes knowing he did it again.

"That's OK, Purple Mouse, you'll be doing that a lot in your life, so don't worry" says Santa. Then he asks Purple Mouse, "Would you like to join Tasha, Mrs. Claus, and me as our very special guest at my Christmas Party tonight?" "Oh, yes Sir Santa! I would be honored to be your special guest!" And then he asks, "Santa and Tasha, may I tell you my story. I mean, how I got here?"

"Why yes, please do," they both reply.

Then Purple Mouse begins, "My mother Orchid Mouse and my father Maroon Mouse were flown here on your sleigh Santa. They hid themselves behind your magical toy sack, holding on for dear life on the back of your sleigh! I saw them fly off with you and then later I ate some of Plum Puddin's pudding and...."

Santa laughs and stops him and says, "Yes, I know the whole story! Remember, I read your Christmas Wish List and brought you the Magical Jar? I have been watching you all your life, from the time your mother was carrying you when they lived at Mouse Trap, to when you were born in Plum Puddin's cabin. I even knew about the mountain lion that scared you and ran you up the roof!"

"Oh Yea, that's right Santa! You know everything. I forgot. Santa, I'm so thankful that you're always on top of things. I hope you've only seen the nice and not the naughty I've done!"

"HO, HO, HO," Santa laughs and then says, "Let me give you a tour of my secret underground lair and then let's head over to Elf Hall for the evening's festivities!" So Santa, Tasha, and a purple faced Purple Mouse have a great time together going through Santa's underground treasures.

CHAPTER 28: SANTA'S CHRISTMAS PARTY

Santa, Tasha, and Purple Mouse are having the time of their lives when all of a sudden they hear over a loudspeaker, "Santa's Christmas Party Festivities starts in 10 minutes!" They look at each other and Santa says, "HO, HO, HO! Let's go!" Purple Mouse starts running toward the entrance stairs when Santa hollers, "Purple Mouse, where are you going?" Purple Mouse stops right in his tracks and looks back at Santa and Tasha and blushes again in his purple color! Then Tasha says to Purple Mouse, "We need to go this other way. Santa has a special exit that goes right through his secret treasure cavern. It's beautiful and will lead us directly to the Reindeer Barn." So Santa walks over and lifts a big green lever beside a golden door that immediately opens and reveals a long tall passageway. Once again Santa says, "HO, HO, HO! LET'S GO!" and they start walking through this hidden tunnel that has even more of Santa's treasures lining its walls! There are treasure chests full and running over of all kinds of gold and riches and there's picture after picture of Santa, Mrs. Santa, Elves, and friends from years gone by. They walk by and see a picture of Plum Puddin' and Pinecone with Santa and Mrs. Santa and Purple Mouse says, "Hey, there's Plum Puddin and Pinecone!" "Yes, answers Santa and then he says, and your picture and Snowdeer's picture will be here someday too! HO, HO, HO!" As they come to the end of the tunnel they discover a big tall staircase that leads them up to another golden door. As Santa opens the door they find themselves in his Reindeer Barn. "Whoa! Says Purple Mouse. What a barn!" "Yes, all my reindeer live here and Harvey my reindeer preparation elf has once again gotten them ready for us to fly off with them tonight for our grand entrance at my Christmas Party Festivities!" "Us? Fly off?" asks Purple Mouse. "Yes, us, my dear friend," answers Santa. "You, Tasha, Harvey, Mrs. Claus, and myself. We'll be flying as soon as Mrs. Claus comes and Harvey comes in and lets us know all is ready."

Just then a door opens and a sweet voice says, "Hello Dear, I'm ready for takeoff. Oh, who's our new visitor?" she asks as she looks at Purple Mouse. "Why, hello Mrs. Claus, HO, HO, HO! This is Purple Mouse, my dear," says Santa. "Oh, what a pleasure to meet you!" says Mrs. Claus. "Welcome to the North Pole. The enchanted land of many surprises!" She smiles at Purple Mouse and winks at Santa 'cause she already knows the whole story, has already met Purple Mouse's mother and father, and has visited with Plum Puddin', Pinecone, Snowdeer and their families. They have all been the talk of the town at the North Pole! She has planned that Maroon, Orchid and the whole gang will be right in the front row when they fly in for the festivities and

Purple Mouse will immediately see them and be surprised!

Then, through the door busts Harvey the reindeer preparation elf, singing as always. "HA, HA, HA, HO, HO, HO, Santa, everything's ready to go!" he says. "Yes, that's great and we're ready too Harvey," says Santa. Harvey gets a funny look on his face as he looks at Purple Mouse. "Hello, I'm Harvey, are you feeling OK?" he asks Purple Mouse. "Yes, I'm OK. I'm Purple Mouse and I learned today that blushing makes me turn purple!" "Wow, that's great," says Harvey. "That matches your name! HA, HA, HA, HO, HO, HO your parents are gonna be so...."

"Uh, um, when you get back home Purple Mouse, your parents are going to be so surprised," interrupts Santa while winking at Harvey. Harvey knows everything that has happened by now. He knows what is going to happen and has just about let it slip. Just about spoiled the surprise!

"Well, are we ready to go Harvey?" asks Santa. "Yes Sir, right this way" says Harvey. So they go out to the loading area and get in Santa's sleigh. In front of them are the excited reindeer busting at the seams to take off. Santa goes over to his Sugar Snow trunk and fills his Christmas stocking with Sugar Snow. Then he and Harvey put the Sugar Snow on all the reindeer and watch as they rise off the ground. Purple Mouse is overcome with joy as he waits to launch Santa's sleigh. He has never flown before and here he is with Santa and his reindeer! Santa gets in the sleigh with the gang and invites Harvey to ride with them.

"What? Really Santa?" says Harvey. "I've never gotten to do your Christmas Party Festivities ride before!"

"Well, there's always a first, says Santa, and from now on you will always ride with us as our Honorary Elf!"

"Yes Sir, Santa! HA, HA, HA, HO, HO, HO! OFF TO THE CHRISTMAS FESTIVITIES WE GO!" he shouts as he hops on board the sleigh.

Then over the loud speakers, Avery Elf announces, "Welcome to Santa's Annual Christmas Party Festivities! Let the Party begin!" And with that, Santa tells the reindeer, "HO, HO, HO, GO!" and they take off at a great speed into the night! Green, red, gold, silver, and white fireworks go off all around them and they hear the crowd below sigh, "Ahh...."

Santa and the gang fly around waving at the crowd and then come down landing directly on the sleigh pad that Russ and Bev Elf have prepared for them, right in front of Elf Hall! This brings a mighty cheer among all the townsfolk at the North Pole village.

Then all of a sudden, Purple Mouse hears a bell ringing. He looks over and sees Strike the Bell ringing his beautiful tones. As Purple Mouse waves at Strike, he sees him light up with a magical light and turn different colors! Then all the elf children's slides light up and turn different colors too!

Santa stands up and shouts, "HO, HO, HO, Welcome! Glad you're all here! This year's festivities will be better than any year before! So grab your partner, and swing along, to the Christmas Party Square Dance song!"

And inside Elf Hall they hear a fiddle and band begin to play. There on a huge beautifully Christmas decorated stage is Melody Elf, singing and playing her fiddle. Dale Elf is on guitar and singing while Josh the singing Elf sings and plays guitar and leads the band. While the song is playing and scores of people enter Elf Hall, Purple Mouse happens to look at the front row, and sees his father Maroon and his mother Orchid, along with Snowdeer, Jim-Buck, Deerlores and family, Plum Puddin', Pinecone, Darrell and Rose Marie!

"Mom! Daddy!" Purple Mouse cries and hops out of the sleigh and starts running toward them. They all rush toward each other and join together in a giant hug. Purple Mouse tells everyone, "My Christmas is complete! I have sure missed you all!"

"Now, the Christmas Party has officially begun," whispers a joyful Santa to Mrs. Santa.

"Yes Dear, this is definitely what Christmas is about," she replies, with happy tears filling her eyes.

CHAPTER 29: PURPLE MOUSE GETS HIS WISH

After all the introductions have been made between Tasha and the gang, Purple Mouse says, "Santa, I have a special request I'd like to ask please?" "What's that, Purple Mouse?" asks Santa. "Well, I left my Magical Jar at the North Pole Mountain and I hope it's still there." "Oh, it is," says Santa. "That's great!" replied Purple Mouse and then he continues..."Well, Santa, my wish is, would you please make it where I could use my Magical Jar and fill it with Plum Pudding and say the magic words like Plum Puddin' says and come up here to visit you, Mrs. Santa, Tasha, Harvey and the whole North Pole gang anytime and bring my parents too?" "Your wish is granted Purple Mouse! Does this wish sound familiar Snowdeer?" Santa laughingly asks. "Yes Sir, it does," answers Snowdeer and then Snowdeer says to Purple Mouse, "I also wished for a Magical Jar so I could come and see Santa but I also wished to pull Santa's sleigh this Christmas and I got that wish too!" laughs Snowdeer. As they are laughing together, Purple Mouse notices something glowing at his feet. He looks down and sees his Magical Jar sitting there and he says to Santa, "Oh Santa, Thank You! Me and this magical jar will be seeing you every year!" "Wow, Purple Mouse, that's what I said to Santa too!" laughs Snowdeer. And as he says that, Snowdeer and Plum Puddin's jars light up too! They all laugh and Santa says,

"HO, HO, HO, Come on, bring your Magical Jars Snowdeer, Plum Puddin' and Purple Mouse and let's all go inside Elf Hall and enjoy tonight's festivities!" So Snowdeer, Plum Puddin' and Purple Mouse grab their Magical Jars all aglow and along with their families, head inside Elf Hall.

CHAPTER 30: GOIN' HOME

What a great Christmas they had! Santa's Christmas Party was the perfect ending of a perfect day for the whole North Pole Village and for Snowdeer, Plum Puddin', Purple Mouse and their families!

As they are leaving Elf Hall, Snowdeer asks Plum Puddin', "How do we get back home?"

"Yea, how do we?" asks Purple Mouse too. Then all the rest of the family start wondering too. Except Darrell and Rose Marie. They already know how to get back because Plum Puddin' had already told them after being at the North Pole so many times.

"It's a secret," says Plum Puddin' laughing.

"Ah, you ain't gonna tell us?" asks Purple Mouse.

"Nope," says Plum Puddin'.

"Ah." says Purple Mouse. "Now that will put you on the Naughty List for sure! Ha Ha!"

They all laugh and Plum Puddin' says, "Ok, I'm just kiddin' you but you have to keep it a secret."

"Ok," they all promise. Then Plum Puddin' says, "Let's get Santa and meet at the Reindeer Barn and he'll get us back." So, they take off looking for Santa and find him over with Strike the Bell in the village courtyard.

"Hello again Santa," says Purple Mouse. "We are having a wonderful Christmas and we sure do thank you for everything you have done for us." "We thank you too Santa," the rest of the group says.

Then Plum Puddin' says, "Santa, Snowdeer, Purple Mouse and all the gang want to know how you get us back home."

"Goin' home?" Santa asks. "You can't go home. We want to keep you here forever! HO, HO, HO!" laughs Santa. "Just kiddin' ya! You can go home anytime you wish! I have two ways to get you home. I can put Sugar Snow on all of you and those who have the Magical Jars need to hold them in their right hand and say, "HO, HO, HO, OFF TO OUR HOME WE GO!" and in an instant you will be back to your homes! Or, you can be taken by me and my reindeer on your own personal trip back to Plum Puddin's cabin!"

"That's the way I always choose," says Plum Puddin'.

They all laugh and Santa asks, "What way would you like to choose to go home?"

They look at each other and Snowdeer says, "We want YOU to take us back Santa!"

Everyone agrees and Santa says, "Then let's head over to the Reindeer Barn and have Harvey get the reindeer ready!"

They all cheer and then Purple Mouse says, "I have one thing I need to do Santa, before we go." And with that he walks up to Strike the Bell who has been watching and he says, "Mr. Strike, it's been a pleasure meeting you. When I come back I'll be sure to see you again!" Then Purple Mouse gives a wink to him and Strike rings back. They all tell Strike goodbye and after being about 10 feet away, Purple Mouse takes one more look back at Strike.

He sees Strike wink back at him and hears Strike say, "Goodbye Purple Mouse." They all turn around looking to see who said that but Purple Mouse just shrugs his shoulders. Santa looks at Purple Mouse and winks at him because he knows that Purple Mouse knows Strike can talk and that it is their secret.

CHAPTER 31: LET'S GO AROUND THE WORLD

When they arrive at the Reindeer Barn they find the reindeer resting in their stalls from a very busy Christmas! The gang looks over and sees Harvey in a corner snoozing away leaning against Santa's trunk of Sugar Snow.

Santa calls out to Harvey and he immediately pops up and rushes over to Santa. After seeing the whole gang he says, "Hello Santa! HA, HA, HA, HO, HO, HO! I bet it's time to take them home!" and then laughs in his forever jolly voice. "Yes, Harvey it is time to take them home. Would you please get the reindeer together and we'll get these folks back to Plum Puddin's cabin?" "Yes Sir," Harvey answers and he goes and gets Gary Elf and Jennie Elf and they pull Santa's sleigh out of the stall and stand it in front of them. Then they get the reindeer and start to harness them together. All of a sudden a thought hits Jennie Elf and she says, "Santa, we don't have enough room for your sleigh to hold everyone! What'll we do?" Then Gary Elf says, "Santa, I have an idea. Why don't we let Plum Puddin', Purple Mouse and the family ride on the deer and let Snowdeer and his family pull the sleigh in front of the reindeer?" "HO, HO, HO! That's a great idea Gary Elf," says Santa. "Santa, may I go with you and the gang on this trip," asks Tasha. "Why yes, my dear," says Santa. "Matter of fact, Jennie

Elf, would you please go and bring Mrs. Santa back so she can go with us too?" he asks. "Why, Yes Sir Santa," Jennie Elf replies and off she goes to Santa's cottage.

So, Santa, Harvey, and Gary Elf finish hitching all of the reindeer and Snowdeer's family together. It made one big long team of deer! Purple Mouse and Tasha hop on the reindeer side by side followed by Plum Puddin' and Pinecone. Then Darrell and Rose Marie. Then Maroon and Orchid. When Mrs. Santa and Jennie Elf arrive, Santa has Jennie Elf hop on Snowdeer's sister Rosie and Gary Elf hops on Snowdeer's brother Deerell. Then Mrs. Santa gets in the sleigh while Santa and Harvey put Sugar Snow over all the deer. Santa and Harvey then run to the sleigh because they see all the deer rising off the ground! The Sugar Snow was taking effect faster than normal! Harvey darts for the back of the sleigh where Santa's magical sack usually is and Santa grabs the reins and sits down. Then he says, "I have never driven this big a team of deer in all my years! We have a lot of deer power pulling this sleigh Mrs. Claus!" he laughs. Then he asks, "Is everyone ready?" "Yes!" they all answer. Then Santa says, "HO, HO, HO! OFF TO PLUM PUDDIN'S CABIN WE GO!". After saying that, the long team of deer dashes forward out of the Reindeer Barn, making their way to Possum Holler, over by Knob Lick. At the North Pole

Marker, the Sugar Snow sees them flying off and millions of them decide to go with them on their trip. So they create a huge gust of wind and blow their way up to Santa and the gang and join them. "Sugar Snow! Welcome!" says Santa. "Let's get these travelers back to Plum Puddin's cabin!" So with a bright glow as they turn different colors, the sugar snow circle each deer, and the sleigh and then fly up in the sky above them to guide them and put on a light show! Then they come back and fly along with the gang. Everyone cheers for them and then Santa announces, "This isn't going to be a direct trip to Possum Holler. Let's go around the world first! HO, HO, HO!" So once again the Sugar Snow circles all the deer giving them an extra boost of power and off they fly around the world with all the gang singing Christmas songs and enjoying the wonderful sights and Christmas lights.

CHAPTER 32: J HESTON COMES TO VISIT

As the Christmas night fades away into a new day, they start to fly toward a familiar looking area. Snowdeer shouts, "Yea! We're home!" As they fly over Possum Holler they see Plum Puddin's cabin. Then Santa says, "Ok, land on top of it." So down they go and as they touch the roof they find they have just enough room for all of them to fit! They all laugh and Santa says, "It's a good thing our team isn't any bigger! Otherwise we'd have had to land on top of Plum Puddin's barn! HO, HO, HO!" They laugh again and Santa says, "Well, my friends, you have made this Christmas one of the very best! Thank you-you all are so special! Well, Mrs. Santa, we'd better get the boys home!" "Yes Dear," she answers. So Santa and everyone hug and say their goodbyes and then Santa says, "HO, HO, HO, OFF TO THE NORTH POLE WE GO!" They wave goodbye and the Sugar Snow swirls around them and they take off soaring through the sky, back to the North Pole.

"What's goin' on up there?" a voice from below asks. Plum Puddin' peeks over the edge of the roof and says, "Why it's J Heston!" Now J Heston is a family friend who is an Ozark historian. He lives in the Ozark Mountains of Branson, Missouri and he's always interviewing folks, writing stories about the Ozarks and putting them out in his paper. At his side, is his good friend, Elias Tucker. Elias is also a writer, historian, and frequent contributor to J's works.

"J, it's great to see you! It's been a long time!"

"Great to see you too, Plum Puddin'", J answers back. "I want you to meet my good friend, and avid Santa fan, Elias Tucker . . . but wow! That was a mighty powerful sight I just saw Plum. Did you see that Elias? You sure don't see that every day!"

"Yea, it was," agrees Plum Puddin'. "It's a special secret between us and Santa, and now with you. We'll be right down. I'll let you in and we'll get a visit in with ya." So they all go down through Purple Mouse's roof door that leads to his bedroom and then they go downstairs and Plum Puddin' lets J Heston in. He builds a fire and they all sit around the fireplace and talk about the events that have been going on the last couple of days.

CHAPTER 33: OUT OF THE MOUTHS OF HORSES

After all the introductions have been made, Plum Puddin', Purple Mouse, Snowdeer and all the others tell their stories to J Heston about Santa and the North Pole Village. J sits there rocking in Plum Puddin's favorite rocking chair listening and taking it all in. Then he asks, "I know you don't want to tell anyone yet about what happened, but can I write down these special events to keep for myself? This story is mighty legendary and I've just got to write it down to keep! Then when we all get old, we can tell it!" he laughs.

"Ok, let's do that," says Plum Puddin'.

All of a sudden they hear hoofs outside on the porch. "It's Charcoal and Brownback!" says an excited Purple Mouse. He opens the door and steps outside and Brownback says to Purple Mouse quietly, "Welcome home. Should we let them know we can talk?" Purple Mouse laughs and says, "Yes! With all that's been going on lately, we might as well tell them this too! You are in for quite a story! So much has happened since I last saw you both!" "We're excited to hear your story Purple Mouse," Charcoal says. So Purple Mouse has them step in the cabin and he says to all, "This is Charcoal and Brownback. They're special gifts we got for Christmas."

"Hello Everybody-welcome home", they both say, and everyone sits there with their mouths dropped open and then they bust out in laughter! "This story just got even more interesting," says J Heston. "When I get back to Branson, I'll be writing for weeks!" he laughs, So, they spend a good part of the day talking with J Heston about their North Pole adventures and J Heston rocks in the old rocking chair taking down lots and lots of notes. They hadn't gotten to bed since being at the North Pole so one by one they fall asleep there in front of the warm fireplace with a head full of dreams of their best Christmas ever.

CHAPTER 34: WHAT ABOUT TASHA?

After they awake, they start talking again about their wonderful Christmas trip. The ladies start fixing supper and Plum Puddin' asks his mother if she would make him some Plum Pudding. While they're talking, Purple Mouse looks over at Tasha and then does a double take. It dawns on him that Tasha stayed with them and didn't go back to the North Pole! "Tasha! You're still here!" he says. "Yes, I am Purple Mouse. We were all standing on the roof saying our goodbyes when all of a sudden I looked up and Santa was taking off!" Tasha replies. "Well, that's alright Tasha. You're welcome to stay here for a while," says Purple Mouse. "But how are you gonna get back?" "I don't have a way unless I go with you, Snowdeer or Plum Puddin' because you have the Magical Jars." "Then that's it! When you're ready to go I'll take you back," says Purple Mouse. "Ok" answers Tasha. But then she says, "Can I stay for a few days and meet some of your friends, and see more of Possum Holler and Knob Lick?" "Why sure," answers Purple Mouse. "And I'll show you Doe Run – where I'm from," says Snowdeer. "That's great! I'd love to see it!" says Tasha. "And you can stay with us here at the cabin," says Plum Puddin'. "I have an extra room here and I would love to have you as my guest!" "Thank you very much Plum Puddin'," Tasha says. So the rest of the week Purple Mouse,

Snowdeer and Plum Puddin' take their special friend around to meet all of their other friends. Everyone loves Tasha and wants to be her friend and Tasha loves them just as much.

CHAPTER 35: NEW YEARS EVE

Plum Puddin' says to Tasha, "New Year's Eve is coming and we always have a big party here at Possum Holler to bring in the New Year. I want you to be our honored guest this year!"

Then Tasha says, "Plum Puddin' that sounds great! I wouldn't miss it for the world!"

"And I'll make you a new dress especially for the party Tasha." says Orchid.

"Oh, Thank You Ma'am," says Tasha.

Then Plum Puddin' continues, "The party is right here at the cabin. Tommy Thomas always plays the fiddle and Ray Elders plays the guitar. My Mama Rose Marie sings and plays accordion, my Daddy Darrell sings and plays guitar and I sing and play the doghouse bass. We'll even have John Fullerton from Branson come over and sing and play guitar! He knows more people and collects more about that place than anyone!" Plum Puddin' says and then laughs. "He'll bring along his pickin' buddies Louis Darby and Earl Vaughan, I am sure! Them boys know them songs like the back of their hand!" laughs Plum Puddin'. "There'll be lots of people come and the cabin is always full! Terrie Young Deer makes the food and Todd Lott always brings the food over in his wagon. My Mama Rose Marie always makes the Plum Pudding," he laughs.

As New Year's Eve arrives, they're rushing around getting everything ready. That evening friends start arriving early and they lend a helping hand with finishing up last minute details. Then at 9 o'clock, the music starts. Tommy strikes his fiddle and the band starts playing. They laugh and dance and eat to their hearts content. As it is reaching midnight, Plum Puddin' says, "Tasha, it's our custom at 12 o'clock that we sing *Auld Lang Syne* and then I give a prayer of thanks to God for the past year and ask for His blessing on the New Year."

"That's wonderful," says Tasha. So at midnight they all shout, "Happy New Year" and then start singing, *Auld Lang Syne*. Then as Plum Puddin' finishes giving his prayer of thanks, they hear a loud thud on the roof. Startled, they all look at each other and then Plum Puddin' gets a grin on his face.

"It's Santa!" he shouts. They all cheer and rush upstairs and go through Purple Mouse's secret roof door to see their special guest. Overwhelmed with joy, they see Santa, Mrs. Santa, Harvey and the reindeer all in a row with Sugar Snow flying all around. The Sugar Snow swirls around each of them, smiling and laughing. In their own little voices they say, "Happy New Year!"

"Wow! This is some New Year's Day!" Snowdeer says.

They all agree and then Purple Mouse looks at Tasha and says, "Are you leaving?"

"Yes, I need to go back. Santa and Mrs. Santa need me to help them at Santa's Underground Lair. But now that Santa has given you your very own Magical Jar, you can come up to the North Pole anytime!" says Tasha.

"That's right and I'll be coming back to see you soon," says Purple Mouse and then he blushes purple. Snowdeer and Plum Puddin' see him blush and laugh so hard they just about fall off the cabin roof.

So, Santa, Mrs. Santa and Harvey go downstairs and celebrate the New Year with the Plum Puddin' Gang. Then after a while, Santa asks Tasha, "My dear, are you ready to go back home with Mrs. Santa and I?"

"Yes Sir, Mr. Claus." she answers. So, they all go back to the roof, hug and tell each other goodbye and watch as once again Santa puts Sugar Snow on the Reindeer.

Purple Mouse smiles at Tasha and hugs her goodbye. Then the next thing they know, Santa is saying, "HO, HO, HO, OFF TO THE NORTH POLE WE GO!" and they all smile and wave as Santa takes off into the New Year's sky. Snowdeer, Plum Puddin' and Purple Mouse watch 'till they were clear out of sight. Purple Mouse says, "God sure dropped a whole bottle of pretty on her!" and then blushes a bright purple.

Plum Puddin' seeing him blush again says, "Purple Mouse, no name could have fit you better!" And then he says, "Come on! We got a party to finish downstairs. And, we've got a lot of plannin' to do for next Christmas Season when we'll go back to the North Pole to see Santa again!"

So they all shout "Yea" and rush downstairs to continue celebrating the New Year and their next trip to the North Pole!

THE END

Credits

Thank Y'all . . . .

Elizabeth Nilges of *"Keep It Simple Photography"*

Josh Driskill Photography (who has been ever memorialized as Josh, the Singing Elf.)

Raine Clotfelter – artist's rendering of Snowdeer™

Dennis Tawes – artist's rendering of Plum Puddin'[SM]

Tonya Lariviere – artist's rendering of Purple Mouse

Jeff Brandt – artist's rendering of Plum Puddin' Productions[SM] Logo.

Terrie Collins – Proofreading, inspiration and additional photography (also memorialized as Terrie Young Deer)

Charles and Freda Carron – thanks Grandma and Grandpa!

Ken Craig – whose name has been changed to "Ken-Buck" to protect the innocent.
Mark Boring ("Mark-Buck") upon whose Cone Chips, Snowdeer™ shall dine in the next volume.

Jim and Delores Plummer – my "DEER" aunt & uncle. (Jim-Buck and Deerlores)

Dale & Melody Driskill whose melodies have transcended real life and emerged in Snowdeer's™ CD and Stage Productions.

And last, but certainly not least, my great cousins: The Krulls, Marquarts, Dorns & Plummers.

Randy at "The Grand Village"
Branson, MO